THESE OUR MONSTERS

English Heritage cares for over 400 historic monuments, buildings and places – from world-famous prehistoric sites to medieval castles and royal palaces, from Roman forts on the edge of a lost empire to a Cold War bunker. By buying this book you are helping us to carry out vital conservation work at our sites across the county so that they can continue to inspire generations to come.

Thank you for your support.

These Our Monsters

The English Heritage
Book of New Folktale, Myth and Legend

Edited by
Katherine Davey

3 5 7 9 10 8 6 4

First published in 2019 by English Heritage
This paperback edition 2024

Book layout: Derek Westwood
Printed in England by Page Bros, Norwich
ISBN 978-1-910907-80-1

MIX
Paper | Supporting
responsible forestry
FSC
www.fsc.org   FSC® C023114

Contents

' ... new matter offers to new observation, and they who write next, may perhaps find as much room for enlarging upon us, as we do upon those that have gone before.'

From *A Tour Thro' the Whole Island of Great Britain* by Daniel Defoe, 1724–7

Introduction

James Kidd

'We will write our answers on paper, and when we return we shall compile the pages into a book.' *Fiona Mozley*

THE BOOK IN YOUR HAND one might imagine as the chronicle of a quest. Eight contemporary novelists – writers of a 21st-century Round Table, perhaps – picked one of eight points around England, each one preserved by English Heritage. As well as absorbing the atmosphere of their chosen site each was charged with recovering the history and folklore that over the centuries have enveloped that location.

The eight stories in this book are the records of those expeditions, which extend from Berwick Castle on the Anglo-Scottish border to Tintagel Castle on the south-west tip of England, from the 12th century to a more or less recognisable present day.

Some of the myths, legends and fairy tales explored by the writers already enjoy rich artistic traditions: 600 years before Fiona Mozley resurrected Sir Gawain's encounter with Dame Ragnelle somewhere in the vicinity of Carlisle, Chaucer's Wife of Bath related it to her fellow pilgrims on the road to Canterbury. The arrival of Tristan and Iseult in Tintagel has inspired works by Thomas Malory in the 15th century and film director François Truffaut in the 20th, the Victorian poet Alfred, Lord Tennyson, and the French composer Olivier Messiaen, the Bollywood director Subhash Ghai and (now) Adam Thorpe. While in Whitby, Bram Stoker channelled his adventures into his seminal novel *Dracula* (1897), as Graeme Macrae Burnet's story reminds us, little suspecting how contagious vampirism would prove. The Count's heirs, including that in Macrae Burnet's story, continue, numerous and infamous: the German horror *Nosferatu* (1922); Bela Lugosi's embodiment in the 1931 film; *Buffy the Vampire Slayer*; Elizabeth Kostova's novel *The Historian* (2005). Others (*Dracula 3D* and *Dracula: Dead and Loving It* spring to mind) would probably have Stoker turning in his grave.

Others in this collection are of more elusive provenance, such as the dancing hare goddess of Salisbury Plain, where Stonehenge stands, who persistently evades the rapt attention of Paul Kingsnorth's narrator in 'Goibert of the Moon'. Similarly the evil 'Redcaps' of Sarah Moss's story, which might be defined as familiars haunting Berwick Castle, among other places on the English–Scottish border, but which were unfamiliar to me.

Together they provide a vivid mosaic of England's pasts and presents. Many of the stories explicitly layer history upon history, folklore upon folklore, rather as the Whitby cliffs formed of millennia's worth of ammonites and alum in Macrae Burnet's story, or the 12th-century origins of Tristan and Iseult refracted through the cut-glass voices of Thorpe's early 20th-century teenagers ('What a lark', Louisa cries) who themselves refract the star-crossed lovers through the stained-glass 19th-century medievalism of Tennyson, the Pre-Raphaelites and William Morris.

The moods of the eight stories are similarly eclectic, by turns comic or uncanny, absurd or scholarly, angry or fanciful, unsettling or poignant. Horror rubs shoulders with tender, if tragic, family portraits. Romances cosy up to accounts of psychological breakdown. An almost Blytonesque celebration of youthful friendship dances around studies of isolation and loneliness.

Navigating this diversity presents the reader with a quest of their own. But what might their goal be? As Mozley's story 'The Loathly Lady' reminds us, quests, no matter how dizzying in scale and scope, are often launched by a single question. That in her own Arthurian update is the perpetually challenging: 'what do women want?' Just in case the task wasn't difficult enough, failure to answer this question satisfactorily results in literal loss of face (or head). Fortunately for Arthur and his sidekick Gawain, there *is* an answer, although it comes with a price, for the handsome Gawain at least: he must marry Dame Ragnelle, undisputed winner of the 15th century's 'most repulsive creature in the known world' competition.

This is not merely the punchline of Mozley's shaggy dog myth; it makes a trial of Gawain's new-found knowledge. Was Dame Ragnelle's secret merely the means to avoid losing one's head? Or did Gawain actually learn something?

What Mozley wittily demonstrates is that the answer, true enlightenment, is inextricable from the quest itself. Wisdom cannot simply be imparted in a few words, but requires effort, by turns physical, intellectual and emotional. Gawain progresses from a state of bafflement and panic about women's desires towards genuine empathy with a perspective that his own chivalric code habitually objectifies, after its own sexist fashion, as alien, comical and, Mozley suggests, *mythical*: 'It is an impossible task; an absurd question without an answer,' that chivalric code initially considers. 'It is a nothing, a nowhere, a never.'

Gawain's journey from this state of bewilderment towards practical, everyday knowledge is mirrored by the reader as they translate the seemingly remote courtly preoccupations into our own time, with its adherence to wealth, privilege and patriarchy. Mozley encourages the recognition of the similarity in the playful opening, which juxtaposes the original 15th-century poem 'The Wedding of Sir Gawain and Dame Ragnelle' with an aside in something like Mozley's own cheeky, sceptical voice: '*Lythe and listenythe the lif of a lord riche* (was there ever another kind?)'.

But to return to the question of the reader's quest, and the question that might spark it: perhaps it is to find what holds these stories together, what they all have in common? But is it even possible to piece together such different times, places and folklore into some kind of wholeness? Bold as such a challenge might be, the pursuit of unity is the very stuff of folklore, at least according to JRR Tolkien, who, in his 1931 poem 'Mythopoeia' defined myth-making humanity as:

the refracted light
through whom is splintered from a single White
to many hues, and endlessly combined
in living shapes that move from mind to mind.

For Tolkien, mythic works provide glimpses of a distant perfection: to 'renew/from mirrored truth the likeness of the True'. Something similar has befallen folklore as a whole, which has itself broken into three 'mirrors' or forms of human truth: myth, legend, fairy tale.

Myths, it is generally agreed, possess a spiritual, or even religious character, and narrate foundational stories in which the mortal world is determined by fate, personified by divine powers. The act of creation can be a nation or a flower, an echo or an entire universe, but it leaves few in any doubt about a supernatural or fictional element. To quote the 17th-century polymath Sir Thomas Browne, they 'containeth impossibilities, and things inconsistent with truth', that is, the hard truth of science.

Legends, by and large, have a surer footing in reality, or at least were once believed to be the real histories of real people, within, or nearly within, human memory – King Arthur, for instance. But as Mozley's Arthur remembers, the act of telling, re-telling and re-re-telling a particular legend over time casts it into a liminal space where fact and fiction merge, rather like the puns on *world*, *woods* and *would* do in Mozley's writing: 'Arthur is everything and nothing, has everything, has no one, wants (for) nothing, desires a world. He is boy-king, man-boy, woods-man. He is king of these woods; he is a king who would.'

Fairy tales, by contrast, are not concerned with gods and with the origins of worlds, or with an at-least possible human history. They have no qualms intruding fantastic beasts and magical beings on everyday reality. This is one reason, perhaps, why they have a reputation as stories intended for children – unfairly, according to Tolkien, as Théoden, King of the Rohan in *The Lord of the Rings*, puts it: 'Songs we have that tell of these things, but we are forgetting them, teaching them only to children, as a careless custom. And now the songs have come down among us out of strange places, and walk visible under the Sun.'

For Tolkien's contemporary the philosopher Walter Benjamin fairy tales were nothing less than humanity's true foundational stories: 'The first true storyteller is, and will continue to be, the teller of fairy tales.' The reason, he continued, was because they liberated humanity from 'the nightmare which the myth had placed upon its chest'. Avoiding the 12 volumes that would be required to unpack Benjamin's ideas on the subject, suffice it to say fairy tales encourage human agency in the face of mythical fate: 'The wisest thing – so the fairy tale taught mankind in olden times, and teaches children to this day – is to meet the forces of the mythical world with cunning and with high spirits.'

But whatever the differences between myth, legend and fairy tale, they share an intimate relationship with the broadly fictional or unreal, which is one answer to the question of what they hold in common. Another is perhaps consequent upon it. For if this slipperiness makes folklore's three major forms tricky to pin down, it does suggest a shared quality that allows them to glide so fluidly through history. If they are not bound by fact, they are not bound by time, either. 'Time slipped and slid around him, unanchored by any fact that could be verified. Perhaps it did not matter.' This is the journalist, critic and poet Ann Wroe writing about myth's greatest crooner, Orpheus. As if to prove her point, she immediately quotes Jean Cocteau's 1950 film, *Orphée*: 'Where does our story take place, and when? ... It's the privilege of legends to be ageless. *Comme il vous plaira*. As you please.'

Folklore's easy indifference to time's usual boundaries – 'As you please' – is celebrated by William Morris in the prologue of *The Earthly Paradise*:

> *So let me sing of names remembered,*
> *Because they, living not, can ne'er be dead,*
> *Or long time take their memory quite away*
> *From us poor singers of an empty day.*

'Because they, living not, can ne'er be dead': it's not difficult to make the leap from Mozley's perpetually conditional Arthur (the 'king who would') across Morris's 'names remembered' towards Count Dracula, who haunts Graeme Macrae Burnet's ominous account of Bram Stoker's visit to Whitby in 1890 – about two decades after Morris began his epic verse adaptation of Greek and Scandinavian myths.

Dracula could be Morris's vision of folklore made flesh (albeit strangely pale): three of the Count's more celebrated powers are his ability to transcend time, defy gravity and change form (from a wolf to a mist to a bat). And while not invulnerable (daylight *can* wreak its revenge), he can regenerate himself by spreading his disease and – in some of the more outlandish adaptations by being resurrected.

In Macrae Burnet's allegory of folklore creation and transmission, Dracula is even more insubstantially fictional: he appears unformed as the spark of an idea, inspiration-in-progress, the glint-in-the-writer's-eye. The 'vampire who would'. His presence isn't seen so much as insinuated through prophetic hints, innuendos and subliminal shivers: 'I felt the blood coagulate in my veins'; 'He has quite turned day into night'; 'and yet when I gaze into the glass I see only myself'.

This pliable draft of the Count's own pliable character is reflected by that of Bram Stoker himself, who arrives in Whitby exhausted, paranoid and 'on the cusp of losing my reason.' This is personified by the 'shadow' that pursues his nocturnal walks through the town. The prime candidate for this 'Horror' is Stoker's Henry Irving: 'I fear that Mr Irving has drained all his reserves of energy and there is nothing left for his wife. In the evening he comes alive a little.' Others include Stoker's own unsteady mental health and his confused, repressed sexuality.

What is really possessing Bram Stoker is vampiric folklore itself: the tales of the Irish Dearg-due told by his mother, Charlotte, the leaches applied by doctor Uncle William and his boss at Dublin's *Evening Mail*, Sheridan le Fanu, author of the famous vampire story *Carmilla*. These are just a few of the forms of folklore that drift from one generation to the next, enticing willing victims (or readers) who, if they fell under its spell, might pass it on, to misquote Tolkien, 'in *undead shapes* that move from mind to mind'.

The tricky question of Stoker's originality, not to mention his sanity, is neatly summarised by the line: 'Whether this Horror is real or merely the handiwork of my imagination I cannot say.' What Macrae Burnet is also emphasising is how Dracula's lifeblood is really stories, transfused from one mind to another. What American shock-master Chuck Palahniuk writes about in his novel *Choke* (2001): 'The unreal is more powerful than the real, because nothing is as perfect as you can imagine it, because it's only intangible ideas, concepts, beliefs, fantasies that last. Stone crumbles, wood rots. People, well, they die. But things as fragile as a thought, a dream, a legend, they can go on and on.'

What Mozley and Macrae Burnet propose is that folklore's forms endure, paradoxically, through flux and persist through transformation. Dracula might be Bela Lugosi, Christopher Lee, Gary Oldman and, well, Leslie Nielsen, but he is always Dracula. 'Time slipped and slid around him, unanchored by any fact that could be verified.'

What might all this entail for that vastest of concepts: truth? What happens when folklore, with its 'impossibilities, and things inconsistent with truth', sits beside fact – and its science, history? It is perhaps a particularly vexed question for our own multivalent, cut-and-paste, post (post (post?)) modernist age of remixing, fake news and virtual reality.

There are certainly many examples of history's material facts in all eight of the stories, not least in the buildings, monuments and sites themselves that provide such atmospheric backdrops: 'The eastern gable of the ancient Abbey, devoid of any protection from the elements, thrust above the horizon like the craggy eminences of the Carpathians' ('The Dark Thread'). The stone circle in Sarah Hall's 'The Hand Under the Stone', each stone with 'bumps, smooth bits, scrapes and chips; each has mountain-copied shapes, like the Castlerigg stones, flat-topped, saddle-backed, peaky; each is booming over or is still upright, has beardy moss or sparkle crystals inside'.

Instead of being monolithic still lives, these testaments to historical endurance are fragile and mutable, and bear the marks of time's passing: Whitby's roofless abbey; the pockmarks in Hall's stones; or the ruins of Tintagel which Thorpe describes as 'like any other ruins: heaps of stone blocks loosely cemented together by a sort of ancient, crumbling mortar into precarious walls, chunks bitten out of them like traces of hungry rats in cheese'.

Of course, what time takes away, modernity also restores and rebuilds. In 'Breakynecky', Moss describes the worn stone steps leading to Berwick Castle, which once 'used to stand implacable against the sky, turreted like the stained-glass Jerusalem in the church windows'. Its current crumbling state is now emphasised by a later bridge, a 'miracle of Victorian engineering', and the even more recent construction work by 'yellow-jacketed men' and their 'yolk-yellow machine hammers'. The perilous climb to Tintagel has been eased, in places, by a 'new, cemented footpath' served by a 'hand-rail that saved any foolhardy visitors from slipping over'.

This ebb and flow is nonetheless grounded in material reality, in the verifiable facts that anchor history. And if historians are a nation's official biographers, then the storytellers of myth, legend and fairy tale are their weird, wild and rakishly enticing older siblings, free to channel the 'vivid flashes' of ancient violence that assault Louisa's imagination in Thorpe's 'Capture' or to hear the whispers of Hall's stone circle.

As Graeme Macrae Burnet shows us, folklore can transform even history's most solid and prosaic artefact into gateways to other worlds and dimensions. Whitby, the unlikely and 'tranquil'town where Bram Stoker discovers his vampiric anti-hero, becomes 'no less than a portal: a gateway to these islands for those shape-shifting blood-suckers designated around the globe as Strigoi, Estries, Jiangshi or Vampyres'.

These different ways to account for Truth are explored by Alison MacLeod in her story 'Great Pucklands', whose opening fuses the language of fairy tale with cutting-edge science: 'At the tangled edge, where bright meadow meets dark wood, hunchbacked fairies stitch the fabric of life ... Bent over their work, they cut, splice and sew with algorithmic speed. Chromosomes split, fray and are re-stitched.'

MacLeod's story is itself a crazy paving tangle of stories,

each with its own very different claims on truth. Charles Darwin's developing theory of evolution, which can be summarised by the recognition that 'We are all netted together', sits fondly beside the vivid, fairy-tale imagination of his nine-year-old daughter Annie, who daydreams that 'hunchbacked fairies stitch the fabric of life'. These ideas can be weighed beside the Christian beliefs of Darwin's wife, Emma, before being set against the poignant biography of the family as a whole.

The resulting hotchpotch map of the many ways in which humans account for their inheritances and heritage is present in Annie Darwin's 'Equations of Ancestry', drawn in imitation of her father's 'lines of inheritance'. So, a brief encounter with 'old carpenter' Alfred Greenleaf, who has 'what looked like a tree-burr growing from his cheek', inspires this equation: 'Conifers – woody flowering plants – Oak Trees – Alfred Greenleaf.'

Annie's hope that fairy wings beat among the bees in Great Pucklands meadow, besides her home at Down House, prompts this observation: '"Larva – Pupa – Slug – Winged Insect – Winged Fairy – Hominin – Human." Fairies and people shared a line of inheritance. Her Equation proved it.'

MacLeod's smart joke is that the amused jolt most readers feel on reaching 'Winged Fairy' would be mild when compared to the utter disbelief that Darwin's *Origin of the Species* would have engendered in 1850, when MacLeod's story is set.

What is more outlandish: the idea that bees have fairy 'bodies sticky with pollen' or the notion that 'The bat's wing ... was related to the porpoise's fin and the horse's leg, and all three were related to the human hand'? A full 70 years later, Arthur Conan Doyle was happy to believe the photographs of the so-called Cottingley Fairies, while Darwin's theories are still disputed by many as fiction, much as his wife did at the time: 'Her [Annie's] mother had explained to her that God made all the animals on the Sixth Day of Creation.'

The search for Truth now presents an obstacle. One interpretation of MacLeod's nicely ambiguous conclusion is that fairy tales offer a fantasy evasion of, if not an escape from, the difficult human truths Darwin was investigating – the ones that lead him to write secretly, 'Old Testament God, vengeful tyrant. <u>Not</u> First Cause', and that prompted 'palpitations and cold, sweaty skin' and possibly undermined his marriage.

This presents a turning point in the reader's quest. In one direction, folklore offers humanity a glimpse of perfection. In the other, it beats a retreat from the contemporary, the modern. In one direction: 'Revolution or Evolution.' In the other: 'Re-evolution.' One might turn again to Tolkien's 'Mythopoeia', whose most conservative declaration takes an explicit swipe at Darwin:

I will not walk with your progressive apes,
erect and sapient. Before them gapes
the dark abyss to which their progress tends –
if by God's mercy progress ever ends,
and does not ceaselessly revolve the same
unfruitful course with changing of a name.

Anyone looking for evidence of Tolkien as a conservative, fuddy-duddy luddite, hopelessly nostalgic for remote antiquity, need look no further. Having blessed the 'legend-makers with their rhyme/Of things nor found within record time,' he says:

It is not they that have forgot the Night,
or bid us flee to organised delight,
in lotus-isles of economic bliss
forswearing souls to gain a Circe-kiss
(and counterfeit at that, machine-produced,
bogus seduction of the twice-seduced).

One hears echoes of this voice in the narrator of Kingsnorth's

'Goibert of the Moon' as he gazes across Salisbury Plain: 'In my mind's eye I see the plain in the times before industry. The hills of yellow grass and green, rolling to a far horizon. The skies clear, the only sounds the birds, the sheep, the wind. Sometimes I curse my mind's eye for what it shows me. All of the unreachable things.'

Unreachable, that is, except through folklore's visions of the hare goddess dancing beneath the moon near Imber, on Salisbury Plain. Such access occurs through a cloud of un-knowing, by forgetting the conscious and intellectual mind. Kingsnorth's narrator defines his childhood attraction to 'Anything primitive or superstitious, any pre-modern notion which cannot be double-blind tested' as 'anything dismissed by the educated as whimsy, stupidity, foolishness'.

Compare this again to Tolkien describing his own faith in folklore: a 'basic passion of mine *ab initio* was for myth (not allegory!) and for fairy-story, and above all for heroic legend on the brink of fairy-tale and history, of which there is far too little in the world (accessible to me) for my appetite'. As Tolkien argued in 1936, this passion and appetite were beyond intellectual understanding: 'The significance of a myth is not easily to be pinned on paper by analytical reasoning ... For myth is alive at once and in all its parts, and dies before it can be dissected.'

This too resounds in the voice of Kingsnorth's speaker: 'The more educated a person is, the less they can really see. When the educated look at hares, if they ever do, they do not see the dance under the moon.' The 'educated' are not alone in the narrator's derision – he pours scorn on the mother reducing the hare to an infantile 'bunny', on chocolate rabbits at Easter and on modern Pagans wandering the Downs waving 'their incense sticks and magic crystals'.

Beneath this pomposity is a deep emotional attachment to this particular folklore and its own attachment to this place. Kingsnorth dramatises this through a later version of the myth, in which Albert Nash, the last blacksmith at Imber, has been forced to vacate the land his family inhabited for generations. On the eve of his departure, Albert sees a vision under the full moon, whose desolate beauty provides a form of release. There is only the narrator's word for any of this: 'I can prove nothing.' But this conviction itself proves how the dancing hare has become something like an article of faith: 'I believe that the hare appears to the grieving, to the worthy, to the lost in soul and body. I believe it comes when it is needed.'

The worthy, it hardly needs adding, just happen to include anyone excluded from society's 'educated' mainstream: 'The lost in soul and body,' which even includes those silly modern Pagans who 'are lost like everyone else', he says in a moment of fleeting charity. 'But why is it necessary to dress up like vampires?'

Again, one can find in Tolkien the same deep solace and even salvation that Kingsnorth's narrator finds in folklore. After the death of his wife, Tolkien wrote to his son Christopher to explain why he inscribed the name of his own mythical character Lurien on her grave. 'I shall never write any ordered biography ... It is against my nature, which expresses itself about the things deepest felt in tales and myths.'

But what kind of consolation is being provided? Ageing, lonely and increasingly out of step with the world around him, Kingsnorth's narrator is happy to proclaim himself one of the lost. Yet does folklore achieve anything other than estrangement from modernity? 'There is a darkness about this world. It is wiser to live alone. Stay silent, walk with your head down. Speak only when spoken to. That way, many of life's arrows may miss you, if you are lucky.'

To be fair to Tolkien, 'Mythopoeia' is an account of private feelings expressed in a private conversation: the poem wouldn't be published until 1964. Its boldness and even defiance was inspired by a debate between Tolkien, fellow academic Hugo Dyson and fellow academic/fantasy-superstar-in-waiting CS Lewis. Despite his recent conversion to Christianity, Lewis was still struggling to understand, among other things, the meaning and purpose of the Crucifixion. Tolkien countered by noting Lewis had no such qualms over similar sacrificial stories in, say, Norse myth, which prompted Lewis to make a famous counter-counter: 'But myths are *lies*, even though lies breathed through silver.'

'Silver' is striking. It conveys the beauty Lewis admits to finding in folklore, while also hinting at its treacherous seductions: a nod perhaps towards Judas Iscariot, not inconceivable given the subject at hand?

The reader's quest presents another trial. For folklore's siren call runs through this present collection too. Moss captures its disorientating allure in those who yearn to hurl themselves from Berwick Castle: who 'long, privately, at the backs of their minds, for a little breakynecky. The general public who yearn, just occasionally, for the vertiginous, for gravity, who crave a slip, a flight, a final snap and smash, whose feet know the way to the edge.'

The superstitious villagers in Edward Carey's 'These Our Monsters' fear their own superstitions but cannot help but sneak a peek: 'Of a general we say no to magicals and satanicals both. True, it does come dark here longtimes and we sit in in the blackness with our little firelights and our weak candlesuns and then sometimes we do wonder about those other things but then in the mornings we always come straight again.'

The pregnant potential of Carey's 'True' is picked up by Hall in 'The Hand Under the Stone': 'Sometimes it's better to not know when something is true. People, including grown-ups, spend a lot of time pretending, to make life easier.' This is Monica, whose preference for writing her name backwards characterises her own folkloric estrangement from her reality. Only, what she believes as 'true' are the myths surrounding the nearby stone circles, which are not simply '*like* a person' (my italics) but actually *are* a group of women, who were punished by a 'wizard who also believed in God' for having a party when they should have been in church. Monica can hear the stone-women whisper to her, something even her Aunty Ro, one of the 'circle-worshippers' who leave ritual offerings in the circle before Christmas, smirks at.

For Monica, an outsider like Paul Kingsnorth's narrator, this capacity to beggar orthodox belief is initially central to folklore's attraction: 'You think about the magical stories, men and women changed, because something in them was different, and they wouldn't follow rules, because they upset people.'

Hall's moving twist is to wonder whether Monica is sublimating her complicated feelings about her brother TJ, whose fragile mental health has cast him further and further to the margins of society. Her belief in the power of the stone circle expresses her increasingly futile hope that TJ can return as the brother she dimly remembers.

Like Macrae Burnet's Bram Stoker, Hall's story deftly mediates between the present and the past, the mind and the body, pretence and cold reality. Hall's crushing final note of almost literal disenchantment is present from the start of Moss's 'Breakynecky', which is perhaps unique in demythologising any form of redemption or even consolation from her admittedly menacing choice of myth. Moss's 21st-century version of the Redcaps who terrorised anyone trespassing the Anglo-Scottish borders starts with a warning fit for a Redcap: 'If you are thinking of leaving, you should probably go soon.'

This, it's soon clear, is no evil sprite, but Mary, a grieving soul stranded far from her homeland: 'It's not my sea. Between the passing of trains, it can sound like home.' Together with her husband, Séan, she fled Ireland destroyed by famine ('There will not be many memorials, at home. Starvation is not heroic.') to find work building 'Mr Stephenson's' bridge across the Tweed.

Granted, there are intimations that the borders exert a special, almost otherworldly, appeal for what Kingsnorth called 'the lost in soul and body', like Mary and Séan: 'We restless ones mass, sometimes, there at the hinge point, the portal where the sea touches the river and the bridge strikes the land.' There are hints too of folkloric transgression of ancient sensitivities. Mary frets about 'disturbing, the ancient ones who were still there when the navvies came with their dynamite and picks'. To which Séan replies ominously: 'sure these are men of science, Mary, none of that', before marvelling at the trains that will make return journeys between Edinburgh and London in a single day.

But Mary now knows better. Experience has taught that the frightening folktales about the 'old man in the tell-tale red cap who lures travellers to his cellar in bad weather' are simply a cover-up for English xenophobia: 'They consecrate their homes with strangers' blood in this land.' Moss's blunt depiction of how an empire remembers its own dead, while exploiting the migrant workers, refugees and slaves who increase its profits, removes any varnish the Redcap fable might provide: 'The English made our men build roads, even when they could barely stand for hunger and it took hours to move a few rocks.' Mary's terse, bitter conclusion seems an act of folkloric atheism that transforms myth into allegory: 'Stones should not fly. Rock is not meant for the air.'

This might be the bleakest moment on the reader's quest, but it isn't over yet. What Moss's story does suggest is a complex and unstable relationship between history and folklore. In CS Lewis's *The Last Battle*, Jewel the unicorn gives a little Narnian history lesson to Jill: 'He said that the Sons and Daughters of Adam and Eve were brought out of their own strange world into Narnia only at times when Narnia was stirred and upset, but she mustn't think it was always like that.'

Lewis's implication, that myth is of most use during periods of national or global turmoil, is borne out by the story of Lewis's friend Tolkien. Born in South Africa at the end of the 19th century, Tolkien was shaped by family tragedy (the early deaths of both parents), constant relocations, religious schism (his Baptist mother's controversial conversion to Catholicism) and two global conflicts: the First World War, which he experienced first-hand at the Somme, and its sequel, which is more or less the period during which he produced both *The Hobbit* and *The Lord of the Rings*.

Take 1936, the year in which Tolkien delivered the British Academy's annual Sir Israel Gollancz Memorial Lecture. Entitled '*Beowulf*: The Monster and the Critics', this was his boldest public articulation of his faith in folklore. One can imagine Tolkien as a dashing knight, shinning down his ivory tower and riding single-handed to save a poem-in-distress (*Beowulf*) from a horde of nasty scholar-beasts, otherwise known as Tolkien's fellow Anglo-Saxon academics.

The specific cause of Sir Tolkien's dispute with the Anglo-Saxon scholars was their savaging of *Beowulf*'s subject matter. While even his most demonic foe (Tolkien respectfully names WP Ker) praised the 'dignity' and 'loftiness' of *Beowulf*'s prosody, his complaint was that it was squandered on such a trashy tale: 'The thing itself is cheap,' Ker concluded primly. Ker and his fellows believed that 'the heroic or tragic story on a strictly human plane is by nature superior'.

But this rather begs the question, superior to what? Enter Tolkien, defender of myth, legend and fairy tale: 'Correct and sober taste may refuse to admit that there can be an interest for *us* – the proud *we* that includes all intelligent living people – in ogres and dragons; they perceive its puzzlement in face of the odd fact that it has derived great pleasure from a poem that is actually about these unfashionable creatures.'

The significance of Tolkien's *Beowulf* lecture owes something to its proximity to the completion of *The Hobbit*, which also climaxed with a battle between men (and, yes, Elves, a Wizard and a Hobbit) and a dragon. But 1936 was unusually volatile even by the standards of that most volatile decade: the Spanish Civil War, Hitler's annexation of the Rhineland and Italy's of Ethiopia, Stalin's Purges, Japan's increasing militarism, the anti-comintern pact with Germany and Italy, the Berlin Olympics, the death of George v and Edward viii's abdication crisis.

Such an apocalyptic context might pose a rather different question about folkloric escapism, which is: why not? Or as Dickens wrote, in a light-hearted, but serious admonition to the caricaturist George Cruikshank: 'In a utilitarian age, of all other times, it is a matter of grave importance that fairy tales should be respected' (*Frauds on the Fairies*, 1853). Dickens's beef with his old friend concerned Cruikshank's injecting of Temperance propaganda into a series of fairy tales, a form that above all others should be free of such worldly sermonising: 'The Vicar of Wakefield [in Oliver Goldsmith's novel] was wisest when he was tired of being always wise. The world is too much with us, early and late. Leave this precious old escape from it, alone.'

One can find a Tolkienesque parallel in the American hippies who flocked to *The Lord of the Rings* in the 1960s and found the 'pipeweed' of the Hobbits conducive to dropping out of mainstream society. But what made Tolkien's work such a cultural force as well as a commercial success was its simultaneous appeal to the politically engaged: the feminist, civil rights and anti-Vietnam movements which tuned into Tolkien's portrait of a small, pastoral, anti-capitalist rebellion defeating a vast, industrialised war machine. 'Frodo Lives!' and 'Gandalf for President!' became favourite slogans of the Counter-Culture, much to Tolkien's public disapproval: 'Many American fans enjoy the books in a way which I do not.'

Similar instability would be reproduced just in time for Peter Jackson's film adaptation of *The Fellowship of the Ring*, whose first screenings occurred only weeks after September 11th. Writing about this experience a decade later, Christopher Borelli of the *Chicago Tribune* recalled the 'queasy jolt of immediacy, a chill of recognition' delivered by Cate Blanchett's mournful recitation of the film's opening lines, 'The world is changed. I feel it in the water. I feel it in the earth. I smell it in the air.'

Similar, if dimly felt, earthquakes produce Carey's astonishing 'These Our Monsters'. Drawing on a 12th-century legend of two green children that appeared by the Wolfpits near Bury St Edmunds, Carey's story feels like a Hammer House of Comedy narrated by Gollum crossed with Alf Garnett.

One can read the story as a tart and timely satire on racism. 'Our skin, to make all right clear, is like any other,' Carey's narrator says, meaning pink, before proceeding chaotically on. 'A little darker in the summer when the sun gets at it and whiter in winter like unto the bones, yes, when it is the winter and the old die before the warm comes back again. Yellowish on occasion due to a sickness, a little blueish if the cold is biting hard. But usual pink like the English we are.'

This reading of the two green children intersects deftly with another: their appearance exposes how the village's sense of community relies on its being hermetically sealed from the outside world: 'We are from here, Suffolk everyone. Been to Bury Saint Edmonds, many of us. Not to London. Not one among us. It is a big place sure. We cannot say what happens there. Not our business. We have no place in it. We do not care for it and seek it not.'

Carey's careful distribution of negatives throughout the story presents an abstract form of clarity ('We' and 'here' versus 'there' and 'not') that is simply impossible to maintain. Some of these doubts are already being voiced. Take the technological marvel that is the abbey in far-off Bury St Edmunds: 'Our first impossible strange thing. But man done it, bit by bit. Took a while. It looks impossible and yet, we have to think about this ...'

This tremor is followed by the earthquake that is the two children – 'otherness' in supernaturally verdant forms. Suddenly, it isn't just Suffolk that is under assault, but the fabric of reality itself: 'GOBLINS ARE TRUE. LOOK, LOOK: WE HAVE

GREEN! WE HAVE GOBLINS AT HOME. Goblins in August. Goblins on a Thursday. Some time between two and three are we having goblins.'

The wild mood grows wilder still as the villagers' certainties are eroded still further in the ensuing frenzy, culminating in questions whose terrifying irrationality resist any laughter: 'But are they children, we wonder? Do we kill children? We think, no, on the whole.'

The reader, hopefully, can maintain a cool enough head to see that the impossible infant monsters are inventions made entirely of the villagers' own monstrous disbelief, which gallops from astonishment to fear to homicidal hatred. 'Though they are no longer in our village, still we think on them. And we do wonder over them. The wondering, you see, comes back thick and fast.'

This is not the first time that the fantastical visions of folklore have been generated by inner turmoil: see Macrae Burnet's Bram Stoker and Hall's Monica. How many of the myths, legends and fairy tales here concern interior mysteries of mind and feeling that are manifested in external forms? This question is perhaps the final answer in the reader's quest, the search for what these eight stories share: the imagination.

In Tolkien's 1936 lecture it was the quality of imagination that he found in the much-maligned dragon in *Beowulf*. 'A dragon is no idle fancy. Whatever may be his origins, in fact or invention, the dragon in legend is a potent creation of men's imagination, richer in significance than his barrow of gold.' The dragon that confronts Beowulf at the end of his own epic quest is, Tolkien concludes, 'A thing made by the imagination for just such a purpose.'

Almost every writer in this book invents a similar 'thing made by the imagination' for their own purposes – the undead 'Horror' haunting Bram Stoker, the beautiful princess in Dame Ragnelle's clothing, the two green children breaking down the walls of a Suffolk village.

In Thorpe's 'Capture', these are the 'vivid flashes' that assault Louisa in the midst of a day whose unexceptional surfaces hide folkloric promise: 'clouds of cerulean blue billowing out like the myth of a Cornish summer.' Like Stoker, Hall's Monica or Kingsnorth's narrator, Louisa is unusually susceptible to the visions vouchsafed by legend: 'huge men covered in dark plates clanking and shouting, the occasional limb sliced through, blood jetting out onto the grass which sprouted on the broken walls as well as underfoot'.

These flashes are vivid enough to transform the otherwise stable reality surrounding Tintagel Castle into something ethereal, intangible, unreal: 'The rushing clouds had brought a giddiness that, completely to her surprise, seemed to be physically forcing her legs away from the vertical and towards some nebulous state that appeared attracted to the waves below.'

Although she is accused of being 'too thoroughly trapped in modern times', Louisa bears witness to ancient scenes that terrify, disorientate and thrill. Suddenly, she believes a *'corner'* of all things 'was pursuing her on thin legs, even though she was going nowhere'. Folkloric imagination shakes time as well as space: turning a short afternoon into an entire 'lifetime'.

Here perhaps is the rejoinder to those opponents of Tolkien who would relegate folklore to a reactionary form. The sheer, unwavering persistence of myth, legend and fairy tale across history offers insight not only into the past but the future too. Having predated us by many thousands of years, folklore will in all likelihood outlive us too, something Louisa senses in the apocalyptic vision of England itself crumbling into the sea: 'Louisa imagined the entire promontory as being swept free of people, followed by the rest of the island of Britain, and then terra firma in general.'

While the land may vanish, its heritage will live on, even if only through the stories passed on of its history, its people and its folklore: the young lovers whose feelings collapse centuries, the whispers heard around magical stone circles, the shadowy creatures of the night that tap at our windows, the ghostly children that symbolise a world, and even a universe, beyond our borders.

All of this, and more besides, has been dreamed up by the eight writers who visited just eight sites around England. Now that they have been recorded in this book, the stories can begin to live all over again.

These
Our
Monsters

Edward Carey

THESE WE DO HAVE: Adam, Aymer, Oddo, Gilbert, Hemmet, Gerolt, Roger, Hugh, John, Ralf, Nicolas, Wilkin and Watty. These we don't: Bonnacon, Basilisk, Chimera, Siths, Fauns, Devils, Leucrota, Ghosts and witches folk. Or either foul things in the forest. Or neither objects that don't obey. Screaming in the houses – that we do. But not little people that are no bigger than a conker. Trees that have voices, never. Hunchedbacked longears – that we do too. Childers born with two heads, a pig with six legs, that sort of thing – no, no we do not.

Not here. Not for us. Of a general we say no to magicals and satanicals both. True, it does come dark here longtimes and we sit in in the blackness with our little firelights and our weak candlesuns and then sometimes we do wonder about those other things but then in the mornings we always come straight again. True, we sometimes have seen a strange smoke or mist rising from a brook and have wondered over if it meant something other than a bit of fog. We do sometimes ponder over the meaning of things, but our wonderings have never given us any solid result only more wonderings. In short, we cannot say for certain.

Now, in truth. Our village is a sensible village. Our village is to be trusted. We are decent people, and God fearing. We should rather it never happened: the particular occasion. We are not proud of it, we would prefer to shun the business and have no part in it. And yet we cannot, and yet we must not. It happened to us and to no other. We do own it. And how upsetting that it should happen to us. Mostly, you see, we are: ordinary.

Our skin, to make all right clear, is like any other. We take no especial notice of it. A little darker in the summer when the sun gets at it and whiter in winter like unto the bones, yes when it is the winter and the old die before the warm comes back again. Yellowish on occasion due to a sickness, a little blueish if the cold is biting hard. But usual pink like the English we are. We are from here, Suffolk everyone. Been to Bury Saint Edmonds, many of us. Not to London. Not one among us. It is a big place sure. We cannot say what happens there. Not our business. We have no place in it. We do not care for it and seek it not.

We hear on a good clear day the bells of the Edmond's Abbey and that to us is the soundslike of great population. Our saint there. Our claim to be close to God. Special people, you see. When go to the Abbey we are with God and we know Him then for the Abbey is so huge and tall and grey and fine and keepout and it worries us and we are proud of it and we know we are small for the Abbey tells us so again and again and we know there is God up there because how else could there be such a colossus? It is the tallest thing in the history of tallness. It reaches to the sky. It prods – very near – the sun. It is a wonder and too long there makes us nervous and we are glad to get away from it and back to things that are a size sensible. But there's no doubting it: that's where God is, the Abbey. The Abbey. Our first impossible strange thing. But man done it, bit by bit. Took a while. It looks impossible and yet, we have to think about this, it was made by people the same size as us. Dreams come solid. See there, Abbey. Hallo, Abbey. And then go home to where we belong where our buildings have no ideas and keeps the outside outside but not much more. Home where the smell of God is not quite so strong and our fear of Him is a little less.

So then. So you know. That is us. Ordinary folk. We also wish to declare: we did not invite them. And yet even so they did come. And so we want to say unto all the world, something that we know and can let all the rest learn by our experience: we know the monsters and strange things are very true. And so: look out. And so: watch you behind you. And so: don't you be alone much. And so: beware please you. And so: we shall never be as we were, never again.

Well then Woolpit, our village is called, get on now, get on. Yes, we are about ready now. Shall we then. Yes. The occasion. The event. Straight forward how.

It was summer hot. Clear day. No wind. So still that something feels not right about it. So still you may hear the faraway bells on such a one. Crops were being cut, reaping men, coming down, gathering up. Fields in stubble. It was one of them fields near some of our wolf pits, which are deep bricked in holes to trap the wolves and stop them coming into the village. It is how our village came to its name. Just there like. One man seen something of a sudden. What's that? There then. What is? I thought I saw sommat. What now? O! Where then? Look! Childers? No not. Like but not! On the edge there. By the wolf pit. Standing there. Two on them. Not children. Something wrong.

Beggars!
Worse than!
We'll have no beggars.
Worse! Worse!
What then?
O, monsters! There are monsters! Actual! Local monsters!

Help! Help ho! Someone yelled. And all come running then.

Had scythes. Brought them.

What strange.

Here in this bit we make a full description of what it was that we found just by the wolf well: wrong, ugly, unnatural, horrid, foul, stinky, lost, hagly, devilbegot, lizardlike. Not Wollpit. Not Suffolk.

Now we have it: the proof of the strange things. Certain. We here captured among our people true, the real, the actual. GOBLINS ARE TRUE. LOOK, LOOK:

WE HAVE GREEN!

WE HAVE GOBLINS AT HOME. Goblins in August. Goblins on a Thursday. Some time between two and three are we having goblins. And will the three bells sound for three of the clock now – or is all halted because of green people? Are we to die now, soonish? Will there never be another three o'clock? Instead shall the sky open and flames pour out? Is the world at the end? The earth tipped? The heavens broke and men are done-fordead? How come it? How come this? Is it true, check then, do check. Close eyes. Yes, that's it our eyes are closed. Then open again. Eyes open. Are they there: yes, yes. LOOK: DEVIL CHILDREN!

Dong a dong a dong a. Time still works then.

They make noise the devilbrood, they shriek and spit, horrible gutter sounds. Whispers of hell no doubt and how they stink, stink like a dirty, rotting place, like mould. They *are* mould we think. Mould in human form. Again we look. But can it be true? Monsters, goblins, childers with green flesh. And help-less too and frightened. They are frightened of us. They do yell. We are frightened of them. We do yell likewise. We are such foreigners each to the other.

What to do then?

With such ugliness, with such newness, with such strange, with such terror before us though yet of childsize and shape. Shove them. Yes. How they fall! Pick them up. Up they get. Shove them again. And down they go! And now? Lock them up. Yes.

We march them to our village.

Done.

What now?

Into the old barn! The old cramped one with no window where we put old Margaret when she went violent.

Done! What now!

Cut them up. What, murther? Yes, pierce gut them, pull out their stinking within and burn quick and then: tell no one.

But are they children, we wonder? Do we kill children? We think, no, on the whole. They look like children. Bit. But very soiled children. Very wrong, very naughty little children. Stained children. No scrubbing the wrong out. Some of us would like to try and it is decided then the women do go about with rags and hard brushes and pumice stones. And do scrub and scrape. But the green no matter how they try will not be persuaded.

To be clear: there are two of them.

To be clear (we have pulled their strange garments away): one is male and one is woman. No hairs between either legs and filthy and stinking. Outhouse sewer childers.

Sharpened sticks are brought. And with these we do prick. The skin is broken soon enough. Red it comes, just a little of it – we did wonder you see.

Ah we forgot to say: they do scream when we do cut them.

Well, is good is not one of us. They pretend most like.

Something else. Their teeth are yellow and brown – and some are missing. Well, so what then, that's as true of our teeth. Yes, that's maybe, but we're not talking about our teeth.

On seeing them, a tally:

Three of us, two women, one man: vomited copious. One of our own children sobs and cannot be silenced until he is taken under his father and given stick, when the stick finds the boy all the more noisome a thick cloth to his mouth does work good. Old Charley: floods his breeches.

Trying to comprehend:

Not child, no, but childsize. We have, we Woolpit people, about us each to a person: arms two, legs two, eyes two, ears two, nose just the one, head, body, all the human things right and correct. Them have, those other ones we mean: just like us, same numbers, only this ... them are green.

Now here we list the greens, for we have been most thoughtful on this colour ever since they did come. Here we are: grass, clover, moss, shamrock, pear, emerald, lime, mistletoe, sea, sparagi, cumber, mint, kelp. And also: goblingreen, uglygreen, humanylikegreen, nightmaregreen, greengroan.

We discuss them in loud voices amongst one another. They have made us very shouty. And some are weepy too. It is not good omen we say over and over. Keep them shut up we think, lock them, they'll quiet in the end. Will they curse us? True, they might. What then? Worst is: we all die. But if we starve them then maybe they will just be good to us and get along and die, quite like. We are wondering loud and severally.

Slice their throats.

Stab them frequently.

Sack them, with stones, in the river deep.

All good ideas, we agree, so we can't decide betwixt them.

So then we return to an earlier thought. We don't feed them until we come to agreement.

Three days. Day One: Groaning, much of. We are firm. Day Two: seem less strange, give some brackish water. Day Three:

they don't move much save to scratch with their long nails on the wall. Their noise scratching nerves us so. It makes our teeth ache. We would rather they didn't. Day four: we can bear it no more, we shall break our secret. We shall tell on them.

Priest then. Yes, we say. Let us bring God in on the argument. We do fall on our knees and weep for God in sight of such a horrid vision. We tried ourselves, us Woolpit, to work it out just private but we found ourselves wanting in such a circumstance, thus we go higher. Thus we go highest, yes so to God then. The priest, the priest.

Our priest, nervous, round, our priest says his Latin. Latin again and again and looks close at the two green ones and tries to work out what they are in fact and looks into his Book to see if the answer is there and drips them with words and holy water. And the green ones look up and mutter mutter.

While our priest is making a decision with what is to be done with the colour green here we stop a moment – thus allowing our priest some time to find an answer – to meantime make open some observations on our own everyday children before the great green came: some are very hairy, some grow spots and die, others turn white as bone and die, a very few have huge strange heads like their brain is too large for its casement, a very few knees that buckle, a handful walk funny, some do not see, others cannot hear, some have no hair, one smell like fish and no body can tell why, one got lost and never could be found, several fall down a well, drowned dead many in river, but never yet green before now.

And the priest? Still thinking.

And us? What do we do?, we ask.

And the priest he makes a decision: feed them. Calls them, perhaps, our guests. Do we sup with the devil now? They may not be devil says he. Let us feed them.

Can we not starve them? We wonder.

They look close to starving already he says. And it is only then that we notice how very bony they are. And there are certainly ribs to these beasts of ours. And it is dead certain what their skull may look like underneath their pelt. Could we open the skin a little further to see if their bones are green too?

The priest he cautions against that.

If we feed them we wonder do we give them people food or animal food. Fit for a person? Fit for a pig?

This is a philosophical statement, Priest says, and he wonders which is the right way. He comes down on the people side and so we get.

Bread, they won't touch it. Though it is such good bread. Old maybe but no one told them that. Good bread it is. Eat up, eat! They do not.

Chicken, little bit. Go on then, eat, eat. They do not. Our wrong children. Right good chicken. How we scrape the floor with our feet at that and shake our fists at them.

Pig then, you pigs eat pig have pig little ham piece piggy piggy but not much. Go on. It's good then, but no. Too good we think. And yet they won't. DO. NOT. TO. OUR. GOOD. PIGMEAT. They make us fury mad.

Turnip?

No!

Beetroot?

No, they don't. Nothing.

What shall we? Such fuss. We kick them then so they know we're not best pleased. And the boy collapses and is very still for a bit but then in the end he moves again. They wish to starve. So then, thin yourself to death.

But then the green girly she sees the stalks of broad beans we have in a bucket. And she starts crying.

Crying for broad bean stalks and so we give and how the boy and the girl both laugh and cry at that. Only they've forgotten how to eat and try the stalks and we show them, show them slow, because they're so stupid and understand nothing of anything. We teach them broad beans. For we know the broad bean, we are familiar with one another. We open them and show the treasure inside. And they look upon us like we've worked the miracle.

And then! And then!

How they do eat. Broad bean follows broad bean deep down into their inner greenlands. And this is all they feel like. Breakfast is broad beans. Lunch broad beans is. They sup upon the broad bean at the end of the day.

Well we say, they are green, makes sense perhaps.

We go off the broad bean ourselves a little from that day.

Then, the next verse of our history, the lord do come. Such is the fame of our green ones. Not the Lord, we're not that famous, but only local famous. The local lord, Sir Richard de Calne himself. The knight, the holder of land. He has heard of our goblins two. He wishes to see.

They came to us, we say, the green ones did. They are ourn, we say. And we stand before the shed, all of us as a wall.

Let me in, he says.

They are foul, we.

Let me in, he.

Small and ugly.

Let me in.

And most of all green green.

In I do command.

And so we pull back the latch. Again the smell comes into our noses.

And so this baronet comes in and looks about. And so there are knighted eyes upon them.

He has a home as big as all of ours put together and with others added too on top of that. Big as churches. But not as big as the Abbey of Bury Saint Edmonds. And lands. Such property and now to add to all this parkland and cows and sheep and pigs and silver most likely lots of we think and now he wants the green ones too. That man he wants a lot. Our green, we say.

My green, he say. You are starving them.

Ours to starve.

For their protection I shall take them.

We fed them. Beans is all they eat. Broad beans, we say. They eat our broad beans, the green devils.

The boy, he says, is most miserable. He is starving.

No, we say, broad beans. We fed them up.

They are dying.

He takes them. Both. Even though the girl is not so bony. Still he'll have the lot.

We shall have more broad beans to us now.

And so we have a change again and see them less. The green people are taken away and we say, good thank you we never liked them you have them then. Not ours, never were. God bye.

We find we miss them. The days drag greenless.

But. And yet. Wait a little. Though they are no longer in our village, still we think on them. And we do wonder over them. The wondering, you see, comes back thick and fast. We wait for more green folk. But they come not. We think about the green children. Who are they indeed? And what? And where do they come from? Tis most strange that they should come to us, no? There must be a reason for it. To come to us, to Woolpit. We want to know what sort of monsters are they, our monsters? What type is that? But Sir R. he keeps them in his great house. And yet we are not all shut out. Some of us do work for Sir R. in his kitchens and dairies, in his stables and smokehouses. And so we get news of our green folk.

They have school!

Goblin school?

And they learn. To speak like they were Suffolk born.

They learn more and more and are become knowledgeable goblins both. Only one of them, the male one, the boy, the younger – it must be the schooling we think – is not doing well. Is mostly in his bed. He has a bed? No wonder then he's failing.

Weeks and months and seasons and no one tells us anything particularly green.

But then the boy is more unwell. But then the boy is most unwell. And then we hear that the boy has died. We blame them. Sir Richard the boy killer. Was living when we had him. Should have stayed with us. To kill a goblin boy like that! He was bony like a fish. More bones than us we think. What a thing to die so far from home. Perhaps, we wonder, they stopped giving out the broad beans.

And then when we think the story is done, a whole two years after, we see her again, the green girl. She's grown older. A woman now. Plump. Ripe. Look there, her skin. What? Not green, is it. What? No, not no more. Pink like us. Is not right, is wrong to lie so. To let your skin tell such tales. Like she was one of us. But we know, we know. And listen, she talk. She always did, grunt and groan, whoops and whistle, squeals and screams. When we poked her. No no, listen, her talks come different.

How so? She talk like us.

She talks.

And we understand.

Is devil, isn't it?

She talks.

Like as one of us.

Tell us then, at last. Tell us truth, if you may. We've been waiting. We deserve to know. We found you after all, we fed you. Shelter we have given. Tell then, do tell.

And, harken, she speaks now. We have such questions. The truth is coming up, from out of her mouth. Words, words.

I cannot tell you where my old home is exactly, says she, only that it is somewhere under the ground. In the ground, deep down. The sun does not rise upon our countrymen; our land is little cheered by its beams; we are contented with that twilight, which, among you, precedes the sun-rise, or follows the sunset. Moreover, a certain luminous country is seen, not far distant from ours, and divided from it by a very considerable river. Nor can I say how we happened to come so lost. We only remember this, that on a certain day, when we were feeding our father's flocks in the fields, we heard a great sound, such as we are now accustomed to hear at Saint Edmund's, when the bells are chiming; and whilst listening to the sound in admiration, we became on a sudden, as it were, entranced, and found ourselves among you in the fields where you were reaping. We never could find our home again afterwards.

So now I am here. What my name was before I cannot remember. And I can no longer ask my brother who you starved. But now I have been given a new name. Yes, indeed. I have a name.

We wait, we wait for the name. Shall it be Samaela or Beliala? Or perhaps Lilith or Batibat? Beelzebee, we suggest, Samalla? Mephistofola, is that it?

Agnes, she says, I am called.

You are green and goblin.

I am Agnes, and I live up at the big house.

You were green once, we know. We know we know.

I am Agnes.

We found you.

I am going to marry Sir Richard.

No! He'd never. Such foreign flesh.

It shall be. I am Lady Agnes. If ever you see me after you

must bow.

    We know you.

    Or be whipped.

We do then close in one around the other of us and is our turn to mutter mutter. There is another world we say, another world deep beneath us. Fancy. Why then does she smile so.

    Agnes, she says once more in case we'd forgot. And she goes. And she never comes again. Not to Woolpit. Other people have her now. She's not ours no more. To take such a woman to your bed! We spit at that and spit and spit and till the taste of the broad bean is in our mouths. We had her when she was green, we had her then. Never Agnes to us. How could she be an Agnes. And we wonder sometimes, if she still favours the broad bean.

    How she did eat them. Like a little monster.

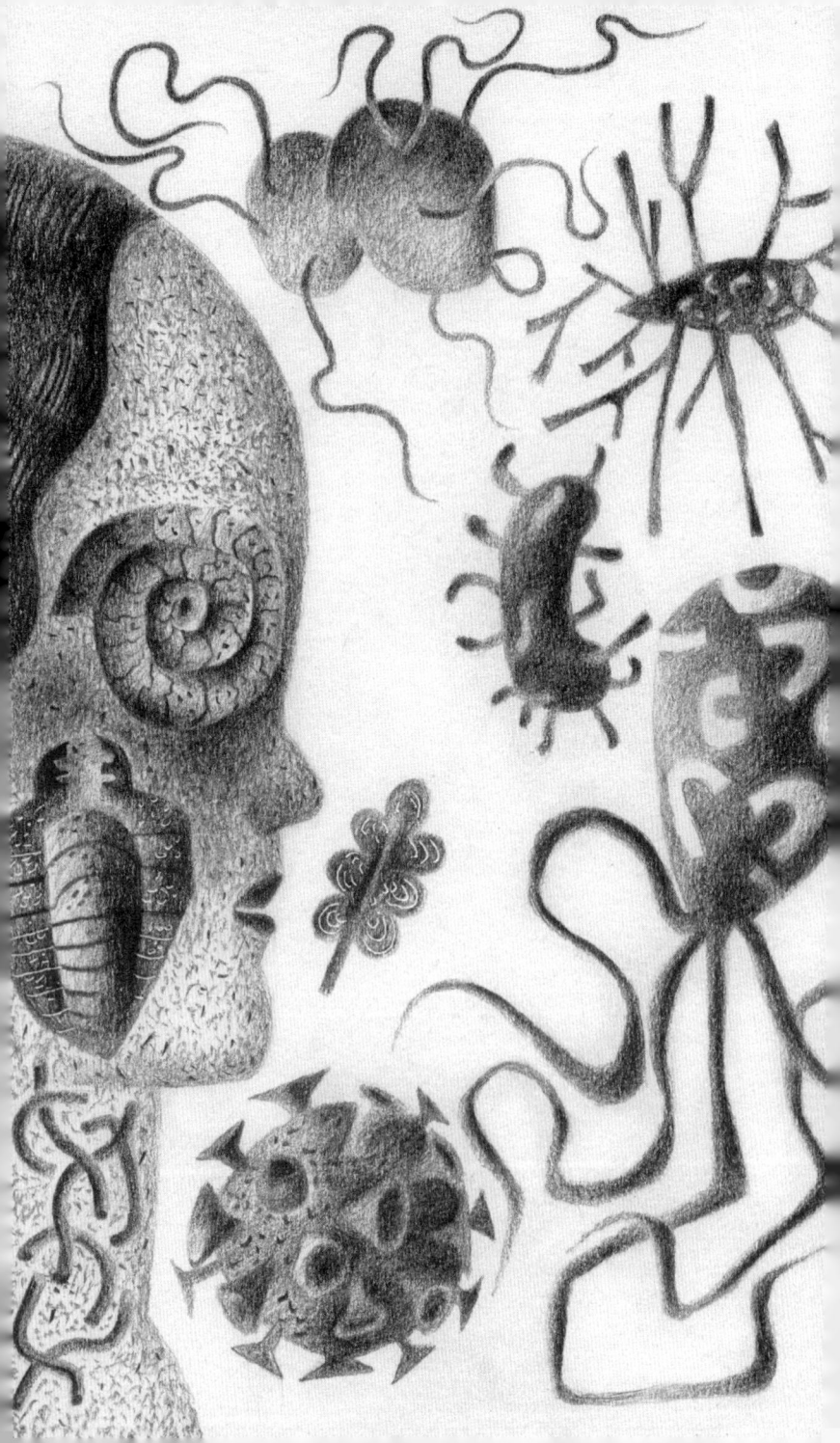

Great Pucklands

Alison MacLeod

IN THE HONEYED LIGHT of late afternoon, they climb, nano-metre by nanometre, from the blooms of Great Pucklands, to flutter on the last of the day's thermals. In the meadow, the air vibrates with the beating of countless wings. *Izz, izz, izzzzzz.*

The fairies' ring is marked by tall, dark grass too sour to tempt any cow. As the bugle flowers blow, they descend. The dance begins. They dip and leap. They link and unlink arms in reels, sequences and flights – over and under, in and out, whirr and whoosh.

Poppy-dust streams. Fairy hair rises, crackling with static. *Izzz, izzz, izzz.* The air is a frenzy of wings.

The bellflowers ring out. Foxgloves tower and teeter. Fair-ies couple and uncouple, their bodies sticky with pollen. Wild orchids open to long-tongued bees.

At the tangled edge, where bright meadow meets dark wood, hunchbacked fairies stitch the fabric of life. Their needles are stingers ripped from living wasps. Their thread is yanked from the cocoons of mulberry trees. A single strand of cocoon silk is a thousand feet long; they unwind each chrysalis to a certain death. *Spin, spin, spin.*

Bent over their work, they cut, splice and sew with algorithmic speed. Chromosomes split, fray and are re-stitched. Genes switch on. Seedpods burst. Saplings spring forth. Bindweed chokes buttercups. A curlew is hatched. Foetuses unfold as tenderly as new ferns; others wither in the womb. Life fizzles and fizzes onward. *Izzz, izzz, izz, izz.*

That summer, the sound of bees in the village of Down was quite extraordinary. On the chalky escarpment, high above Cudham Valley in the North Downs, a loud buzzing arose from Great Pucklands. Only Anne Elizabeth Darwin – Annie – aged nine, and her father understood that the sound was too loud for bees alone.

He emerged from the village shop, gripping castor wheels for his microscope-stool. 'Spied any yet?'

She shook her head. 'But I hear them. Have you, Papa? Seen any?'

He said he wasn't sure he wanted to see them. Fairies weren't always pretty mites. That was just tales people told for babies.

'But you do have your beetle jar,' she said, 'in case we see one?'

He patted his jacket pocket reassuringly, then passed her a liquorice string. She jumped joyfully, calling to mind a rhinoceros he'd once seen in the Zoological Gardens in London. Its keeper had let it out of its pen into the sunshine, and the rhino had kicked and bucked with irrefutable joy.

We are all netted together, he thought.

'We might see one on the way home,' Annie ventured.

'A beetle or a fairy?'

'Both, perhaps!'

At St Mary's lych-gate, she turned a cartwheel, and her locket slipped from her chest and knocked her forehead. She righted herself and grinned.

Alfred Greenleaf, the old carpenter, passed at that moment, tipping his hat. 'Afternoon, Mr Darwin.' Alfred had what looked like a tree-burr growing from his cheek, and Annie stared, delighted, until her father hauled her on.

***

At Down House, she ran up the stairs to the nursery and leaped over the deep dip in the boards at the top, the warp which the children knew as 'The Bottomless Hole'. No matter how fast they ran, they knew to step over or around The Bottomless Hole and never *into it* – lest they go down, down, down, forever.

She arrived, sweaty, at her desk and entered her Equation of Ancestry in the paper book she had made and stitched herself: 'Conifers – woody flowering plants – Oak Trees – Alfred Greenleaf.' She made each of her letters carefully, adding curls to her capitals.

Her father was teaching her about lines of inheritance. Sometimes, when she was poorly or tired, she was allowed to rest on the couch in his study while he did his barnacles. Then he would take down from his shelf *The Zoology of South Africa* and let her turn its pages. She loved the drawings of the primitive hominins and monkeys best.

She paused at her inkpot long enough to allow Brodie, her nurse, to scrub the liquorice from her face. Then she added another Equation she'd devised: 'Larva – Pupa – Slug – Winged Insect – Winged Fairy – Hominin – Human.' Fairies and people shared a line of inheritance. Her Equation proved it.

Annie had three things of her own: a locket, given to her by her mother, which waited for something to close inside and wear by her heart; a beautiful barnacle shell from New South Wales, given to her by her father; and a new wooden writing-box, given to her by her parents for her ninth birthday.

The writing-box was covered in morocco leather. It was a smaller version of her mother's writing-box, with a hinged lid and compartments inside lined with crimson paper and gold stars.

Having completed her newest Equation, she closed her jotting-book and locked it inside her writing-box. Then she took the writing-box's tiny key and closed it in her locket.

That night, with her head on the bolster she shared with her little sister Etty, she asked her father which genus of tree Alfred Greenleaf shared an ancestor with.

'Which would you say?'

'Oak. Or possibly Copper Beech.'

He laughed and thumped his leg, a sign, Annie told herself, of his pleasure in her Equation. Then he explained that her locket was for daytime only. He unfastened it gently where it was caught in her hair and kissed her goodnight. Cracks of light from the shutters made it hard to close her eyes. She stared at her barnacle shell, and then it was morning again.

At Down House that June, there wasn't a breath of air. The grass was burnt brown. Great cracks had opened in the ground. Between the two old yew trees, the swing hardly moved.

Brodie, Miss Thorley, the governess, and her mother carried fans wherever they went. Their fans, when opened, were as splendid, Annie thought, as the wings of bats.

She knew because one evening, a few weeks before, her father had laid out his specimen trays for her on the floor of the nursery. Bones were pinned into place on sheets of cork. The bat's wing, he told her, was related to the porpoise's fin and the horse's leg, and all three were related to the human hand. 'Can you see?' he asked.

She fingered the bones and nodded. Then she ran to the nursery desk where she wrote her very first Equation in her paper book: 'Bat – Porpoise – Horse – Human.'

Her father nabbed her nose. 'Not a word to your ever-loving Mama.'

'About bat wings and hands?'

'About bat wings and hands.'

Neither of them wanted to make her cry.

Her mother had explained to her that God made all the animals on the Sixth Day of Creation. She'd explained that, when the Flood came, Noah saved the animals, taking them into the Ark two by two, which was why they were still with us today, just as God had made them. She'd smiled and walked the four fingers of both hands along Annie's legs.

Her mother re-told the story when Etty and George were old enough to sit still. 'Did Noah take the intermediate species too?' Annie asked at the end.

Her mother looked at her hands. Her forehead crinkled. She said little girls and boys needed only to love and delight in the Word of God, and she cut out paper animals for them, two at a time. She made excellent bears and lions, but pigs, they all agreed that day, were her masterpieces.

It was midsummer 1850, the bright beautiful hinge of the summer and the century – and another scorcher of a day. Croquet mallets, hoops and tennis racquets lay strewn across the lawn, like mismatched skeleton parts. Three of the children stretched out as well, sweaty and sunburnt on the grass, with starfish arms and legs. Willy was not yet home for summer from Mr Wharton's School, and Betty and Francis were too little to play out in the sun.

Faces to the sky, Annie, Etty and George sucked nectar from the sage flowers they'd stolen from the kitchen garden. For a time, they listened to Parslow, their father's man, draw water from the well in the service yard. *Skr-eeee*, *skr-eeee* went the fly-wheel.

Their mother, Miss Thorley and Brodie picked up their cane chairs and moved them away from the noise, into the shade of the Horse Chestnut. Their mother was beautiful in her lilac muslin. They watched her shoo a bee and pour the tea.

Ladies weren't allowed to *make* a pot of tea, Annie explained to Etty and George, unless they were Mrs Davies the cook. Ladies couldn't post a letter or ride in a train carriage by themselves. Nor could they go out in the dark alone to watch for owls, badgers or shooting stars. That's why she was never going to be a lady. Her mind was made up.

Etty said she *might* become a lady if she didn't have to ride a pony side-saddle. Annie said she never would. George said he never would either, and, in solidarity, laid his small head in Annie's lap.

Skr-eeee, *skr-eeee*. Poor Parslow. The flowers were wilting in every bed, their father was poorly and needed buckets and bucketsful every day for his water-therapy, and there was never water enough for the house. Mrs Davies shouted and the maids simmered in the heat.

On Mrs Davies' stove, a vole also simmered, making the kitchen smell foul, which did not improve Mrs Davies' temper. Later, Annie and her father would strip it down to its skeleton and pin it out.

That summer, her father's Great Secret also simmered. His special Equation. His Origin. The one he scribbled when her mother thought he was doing his barnacles; the one that gave him palpitations and cold, sweaty skin. He wrote it down on scraps of paper and hid them in his table drawer, in his coat pockets and under specimen jars, as if he were hiding them from even himself.

The wide Kent sky was a lid on the pot of Down House that summer. *Bubble*, *bubble*.

On the parched lawn, the children turned onto their bellies and watched their father pace the long perimeter path. The Sandwalk. He was on the third lap of his five. His 'constitutional'. Twice a day. Sometimes they'd sneak up and steal one of the stones he deposited with every lap – to throw him off his tally. He was always deep in thought, pondering the vast, empty wastes of Patagonia or the savages of Tierra del Fuego, all of which he'd seen before any of them were born.

Now as they watched, he bent down – to study an ant

at work or perhaps a slug not at work. The earthworms had burrowed deep in the earth because it was too hot. When he straightened, he raised his walking-stick high in a salute, and they waved back.

All the while, Annie listened. Above her father, in the canopies of the lime trees, the fairies droned, like one great, mournful harmonium. She suspected they knew about his butterfly net in the cupboard under the stairs. They knew something. The longer he lingered by the lime trees, the louder the noise of their wings. *Izzzz, izzzzz, izzzz.*

When Annie was born on the 2nd of March, 1841, her father, Charles, had weighed and measured her, as he would each of his 'animalcules' in turn. It was a difficult birth, and as a babe-in-arms, she was frail and a worry.

Her first smile arrived, Charles recorded, on her forty-sixth day, and others followed effortlessly and often thereafter. Her first word was 'goat', and Charles rejoiced. Emma still fretted, however. Their firstborn, Willy, had been declared as an infant a 'prodigy of beauty & intellect' by his father, and Emma herself had fallen in love for the second time in her life. But when Annie was nine months old, Emma confided to her diary, 'She is very ugly, poor body, with a broken out ear just like mine.' Later that year, she wrote to her aunt, 'My little Annie has taken to walking and talking for the last fortnight. She is thirteen months old and very healthy, fat and round, but no beauty.'

Charles delighted in cuddling and kissing her. She wrinkled up her nose when she smiled or didn't understand. She would appear with blades of grass torn from the lawn for him. When she reached fourteen months, he marvelled that she took hold of pens and pencils 'in the proper way'. When she was two and three-quarters, Emma put little combs in her hair, and Charles declared it made her look *quite a beauty*. Soon, she'd arrive in his study, grinning and proffering a pinch of snuff from the jar in the hall from which, she knew in her own childish way, he was meant to abstain. Never, he announced to Emma, had there been a more affectionate child.

Now, aged nine, Annie was sometimes allowed to help Mrs Davies with grown-up things. One afternoon, as she collected the teacup and orange peels from her father's study, she stopped short at his armchair and frowned. His scraps of Theory were multiplying. She could see them hiding around his study, like clues to a terrible treasure hunt. They were words that would worry her mother and send her father to his bed again.

One poked out from behind a cushion. She read it – 'Species not immutable, though like murder to confess it.' – and she snatched it up.

Another fluttered on the floor below the window: 'Animals are our fellow brethren. Man is not demeaned when compared – on contrary, animals have cause to object!'

She herself found their donkey and Bran, their terrier, every bit as nice as Etty and George, but she knew it wouldn't do for her father to write that down in a book, even if he agreed, which he did. The vicar at St Mary's would get very cross.

On the drum-table, under a jar of barnacles, she found the worst yet: 'Old Testament God, vengeful tyrant. Not First Cause.'

Her mother would certainly cry at that.

She took the scraps, smoothed them flat, and ran upstairs, leaping as always over The Bottomless Hole. Then she shut them in her writing-box, turned the key and closed the key in her locket.

At the open window, fairies hovered, watched and buzzed. *Izzzz, izzzz, izzz.*

Her father told all his children that questions were very good things, and that it was better to know nothing than to know everything. Annie wrinkled her nose. She wanted to know *why*. That was her question. Because she wanted to know everything.

She stood in his study, waiting for his answer. He took a seat on his microscope-stool, meeting her at eye-level. He said that he, for example, knew *how* life was but not *what* life was. *That* was the great mystery. His own vexing question. 'What is the *Is* of Life, Annie? No one knows!'

She shrugged, impatient. She had another question, she said. She wanted to know if Mary Eleanor, her baby sister who had died at three weeks, was with the angels in Heaven. Her father cleared his throat to speak, but, at that moment, her mother passed in the hall outside the study, and her father stopped.

Why, she demanded, would he talk about fairies perfectly sensibly, but never about angels? He tried to tickle her but she stamped her foot in a rare display of grievance. Then her mother called her and the other children into the drawing room and proceeded to play The Galloping Tune very loudly. Annie sat straight-backed on the chaise-longue and would not join in.

That evening, her father found her in the nursery under the quilt. Later, in his notebook, he would ask himself: 'Children & hiding & hiding games: vestige of savage instinct?'

He drew her onto his lap. 'Are you crying, Kitty Kumplings?' He had called her that since she was a baby.

'No,' she said sadly. 'It's only water coming from my eyes.'

She buried her hands in his shirt and chest hair. He growled on cue for her like a bear, if quietly because Etty and George were already asleep.

Her mother joined them and read softly from *The Nursery Rhymes of England*, adding a rhyme from her own girlhood, 'There Was an Old Woman as I've Heard Tell', which was Annie's favourite. The vicar, her mother said with a wicked smile, did not approve of nursery rhymes. He thought them 'immoral'. But vicars, she said, did not know *everything*, and neither, for that matter, did mamas or papas. She did know, however, that Mary Eleanor was safe with God. There were truths one knew in one's head, and truths one knew in one's heart.

Her father said her mother was eternally wise, and they kissed Annie goodnight. Then they went down the stairs for their nightly game of backgammon.

What things did mothers and fathers *not* know? Annie found her father's list on his Pembroke table.

'Why do men have nipples?'

'What can be the origin of movement from tickling?'

'What is emotion?'

'Why does joy and other emotion make grown-up people cry?'

'What passes in a man's mind when he says he loves a person?'

She knew the answer to the last one. What passed in *her* mind was the tickle of her father's whiskers as he kissed her goodnight, and her mother's smooth hand on her forehead when she was unwell.

What passed in her mind was sitting on her father's lap on his microscope-stool, and clinging to him as he punted them through the drawing room with his walking-stick. What passed in her mind was Mama not caring that the wheels scored the carpet.

She remembered, too, her father's laugh as he slid on his bottom down the sliding-board that fitted over the stairs. He'd had old Alfred make and polish a sheet of wood, with hooks to fit it to the top stair and the bottom. Even Mama and Miss Thorley took turns on the slide; their crinolines made them go very fast. But only Annie could do what the family called 'Eight Stairs Standing'. She glided all the way in her stockinged feet from top to bottom. She felt like a shooting star.

More than anything, what passed in her mind was the Secret she kept for her father: that he did not believe in angels or the Bible. Perhaps not in Heaven either. The vicar once said a person must believe in Heaven to be admitted to Heaven, and Annie had seen her mother look mournfully over the row of their Darwinian heads to the unhappy shape of their father, who looked poorly and clutched his stomach.

The doctor said her father's illness was 'dyspepsia'. Her mother told the doctor she was confounded by the range of his symptoms. Parslow scrubbed and showered her father daily for his water-therapy, but he was often ill and brought up his food.

Annie knew his Secret was the First Cause of his poorliness; that it made his heart flutter, his head ache and his legs give way. It made him rush to the privy, bent double, and take to his bed for weeks at a time. It made him tremble and weep in Parslow's arms, unable to stop, even when she and Etty stood, wide-eyed, at his bedroom door.

The long hot spell of midsummer broke at last. Thunder and lightning split the sky over Down House. The storm arrived on the day Charles felt well enough to leave his bed and lock himself away in his study to write once more. The air cleared.

It was the day that Annie stepped into The Bottomless Hole.

Etty and George had been running behind her up the stairs when their sister collapsed in a heap at the top, outside the nursery. They froze where they stood and Annie began to cry strangely. Etty shouted for Brodie, who arrived in a rush of black silk, and scooped Annie up. Brodie muttered that she hadn't been herself all day. 'Who has she been, Brodie?' asked George, but their nurse had already disappeared, with Annie limp in her arms.

It was the summer Annie began to weaken and fail.

Down, down, down, she went.

She weakened, rallied and weakened again.

Charles and Emma lived for months in a place of dread from which they would never fully return, a place more remote than the wastes of Patagonia.

Annie died on the 23rd of April, 1851.

Charles' words would swim back at him nightmarishly from his notebook: 'There is a ceaseless and incalculable waste of pollen, eggs and immature beings.'

Cause of death: 'bilious fever'.

In Great Pucklands, the hunchbacked fairies stitched and cut, stitched – and cut.

She was buried with her locket at her breast and her barnacle shell tucked in her fingers.

Down House fell into a profound silence.

On a high shelf in the nursery, her writing-box sat, locked and forgotten, under a film of dust.

But beneath its hinged lid, the darkness metabolised. Over the days, nights, weeks and months, the crimson of the paper lining deepened like an expectant womb.

The stitches on the spine of her book began to strain and pull.

The ink on its pages grew wet again to no one's touch.

Her curled capitals flexed, rearing up.

Then her beloved Equation broke free of its line and transmuted on the page before no one's eyes. 'Larva – Pupa – Slug – Winged Insect – Winged Fairy – Hominin – Human.' It flickered to life, in a bright kinetic reel, a candescent chain of life, while outside the nursery window, fairies swarmed.

They flew at the panes, their wings beating the glass.

Izzz, they sang, *is*, *is*, *is*.

Goibert
of the
Moon

Paul Kingsnorth

THE CHILD'S NOSE was pressed up against the glass display case, his dirty little fingers smearing whatever muck he had last eaten all over it. The condensation from his breath obscured what was on the other side. It made little difference to him, as he was clearly unable to concentrate on anything that wasn't featured on the screen of a phone.

'Do you like the bunny?' asked the boy's mother, cradling another, smaller, brat in her arms. It wriggled like a worm on a hook as she spoke. 'Isn't it cute?' she added, hopefully.

The child stared through the steamed glass at the stuffed hare for perhaps five seconds, and then wandered over to the fox and the badger, which are even scrawnier and less shapely after a century in a museum case. The mother smiled at me wanly as she followed him. *It's a bloody hare!* I felt like saying to her. *It's a hare, not a 'bunny'. Can't you see the difference? Set your snivelling little child an example!* I did not say this. I only nodded. I have found as I have grown older, much to my delight, that it is possible to get through most days without having to say anything to anyone at all.

After the child had left, I produced my handkerchief and carefully cleaned the glass. European Hare, read the Victorian

61

hand-lettered label. *Lepus europaeus*. I looked into her glass eyes. Her black-tipped ears were balding, as if she had mange.

Old side-looker, I whispered to her, through the glass. *Stag of the stubble. Old Turpin. They have never treated you as you should be treated. No respect. There is no respect left in this world. Left on show here as if you were just another beast of the fields. As if you were mortal. But I will find you. I am still looking.*

I try not to talk to the hare when there are others present.

The museum is not far from my home. I come here perhaps once or twice a week. The staff are used to this eccentric old man wandering through their exhibits. I do not care how they see me. The hare knows me perhaps better than any human. I come because I feel, sometimes, as if looking into the eyes of the hare – false though they are – may furnish me with answers to questions which my research in more conventional areas has so far failed to reveal. I realise this is superstition. This is why I do it. Since I was a child I have gravitated towards anything dismissed by the educated as whimsy, stupidity, foolishness. Anything primitive or superstitious, any pre-modern notion which cannot be double-blind tested. The more educated a person is, the less they can really see. When the educated look at hares, if they ever do, they do not see the dance under the moon. They do not see the transformation. They do not see what She is and can become. The power and the danger, the polar dance on the green downs in summer.

No. They see a bunny.

But the dance continues, I am sure of it. Up there some-where, in the old, high places. Before I die, I will bear witness.

fire rises in the circle
fire rising up the stones
the stones dance as if they are alive
they are alive
above the circle, the moon's eye watches
the order of things shall be as ever

and the people stand circled within the ring
and the coals are the colour of the blood moon
and all speak now the words of summoning

the hare is brought forth

The hare's association with the moon is of particular interest to me. The hare that dances on the plain here appears when the moon is full. This is what the tales say, in what scant documentary evidence remains. It was often the case that hares seen when the moon was full were considered to be bad luck. In many parts of the country, in fact, hares were bad luck at any time. In the West Country, no fisherman would put to sea if he came across a hare on the way from his home to his boat. Once at sea, any mention of the hare was strictly forbidden. Take a hare aboard your vessel and drowning is certain.

The moon hare is not a purely British phenomenon, which interests me greatly. The association is global. Silimukha, the Indian hare-king, is connected with the moon. In China, a hare sacrificed itself to the Buddha by throwing itself onto a fire. The Buddha, in recognition of its offering, commanded that the hare's image should henceforth adorn the disc of the moon. The moon is a hare in many lands, and the hare becomes the moon in many others. Moon-hare tales lurk in the mythologies of Morocco, South Africa, France, Russia, various American Indian nations. There is a strange image of what appears to be a hare goddess in an old Saxon text. The Celtic goddess Ceridwen is linked also with hares. The Egyptian moon god Un-nefer, an early manifestation of Osiris, king of the dead, became a hare at the correct time of the month. And what of the hares painted high up in the Paleolithic caves in the Dordogne? What of the hares on the shaman's drumskins in Lapland?

The hare lives in the places between. She is never merely animal. All have known this.

All except us.

The hare and the moon: across the world, they saw the connection. Back when the outer world was alive, when Man was not the measure of all things. Back when we could see beyond the ends of our noses. Before the lights came on and the asphalt went down. They all saw something. Here, when the moon was full, many times over the centuries, they saw the hare dancing on the plain, near the henge. The circling hare that came with a message. What did it have to say?

silence is the sky
silence in the moon's eye
still the stones dance
and now the people hum
and the hare is brought to the fire
and the herbs are brought to the fire
and the oil is brought to the fire
and the hare annointed
it does not struggle
its ears lay flat upon its skull
in my arms now it is still

my arms now I raise to the fire
the hare does not move
in its eyes the flames dancing
Become, I say
Become!

The old church at Imber is only accessible now on a few days each year. A strange place, is Imber; strange and sad. A high, lonely village up on the plain, it was requisitioned by the War Office in 1943 and the villagers expelled. They were never allowed to return, even when they descended *en masse* and demanded their homes back. Their homes are long gone, the thatched cottages, the inn, the manor, all replaced by concrete block houses where soldiers can practise kidnapping, killing, raiding, whatever it is they do and wherever they do it. But the church still stands, and once a year the public is allowed to visit. It has been stripped of its fittings – the pews are gone, the altar, the font. But the ghosts are still here.

It is in the parish records of St Giles' at Imber that the hare first appears. The date is 1318. John Godwin, a shepherd on the plain, was on his rounds. Where he was precisely is not known; or was not known, before my work began. It was somewhere between the village and the henge, which is perhaps ten miles distant. It was the evening of the full moon, and the shepherd was resting on the downs. In my mind's eye I see the plain in the times before industry. The hills of yellow grass and green, rolling to a far horizon. The skies clear, the only sounds the birds, the sheep, the wind. Sometimes I curse my mind's eye for what it shows me. All of the unreachable things.

Godwin was resting, evening was coming down, when a hare appeared before him. I don't suppose he paid it very much attention until it began to circle him. Clockwise it went, according to the records. It circled him continually, watching him always from its side-on eyes. Perhaps the moon was rising. The hare continued circling the shepherd, but now it began to stamp its hind legs as it did so. Its speed seemed to increase with every circle it made around him, the stamping got faster. The hare appeared to be dancing in a circle around the shepherd, who sat, barely breathing, simply watching. And then the moon was high and the hare was gone and John Godwin was hurrying back across the plains of grass to Imber, to tell his neighbours what he had seen. Godwin's wife had died earlier that year; his one daughter just two years before her. As he moved over the plains in the brightening moon, his heart felt somehow lightened for the first time in years.

This is what I see.

What we don't know is whether John Godwin was the first to see the dancing hare of the plain, or whether he was merely the first to record it. I favour the latter theory. I believe the hare's dance is very much older than any records we have access to. I believe it may date, even, to the times when the henge was in use. Can the henge's proximity to the site be coincidence? It could, but I doubt it. The whole plain is a great magical landscape, perhaps the pre-eminent one in these islands. I have no evidence upon which to base this theory. All I have is a hunch.

now with flames rising
sound of the circle rising
moon rising
I step to the fire
raise the anointed one in my arms
ears down, eyes wide
power in her stillness
Become! I say again

I offer her body to the flames

From the fourteenth century onward it is possible to track the dancing hare right up to the present. In parish records, in newspaper reports, in stories passed down through families, claims are made by those who have seen, or believe they have seen, her dancing up high when the moon is full. From the middle of the twentieth century the reports decline – partly, I suspect, for fear of appearing superstitious, partly due to the decline of rural culture and partly because the Army's colonisation of the plain made her territory inaccessible to the unarmed. Still, in the late 1960s a local newspaper gives us the tale of another farmer, out in his fields one full moon night, who met with the hare and witnessed the same dance that John Godwin had witnessed six hundred years before. This farmer, it seems, had also recently lost his wife.

I may as well say what I think at this point. I may as well

lay out my theory about this dancing hare, drawn from my years of research. As I say, nothing can be proven. I speak about this to few people, and not only because I speak to few people about anything. But I believe that the hare appears to the grieving, to the worthy, to the lost in soul and body. I believe it comes when it is needed. I believe its dance is an offering, as old as time. In some way, I know this. In some way, in some way, I have seen it before.

Do not ask me to explain anything.

the hare does not draw back
the music of the circle grows louder
the flames are high
the stones dance
the hare kicks in my arms
its back legs thump into my breast

it leaps in to the fire

There is a rather wonderful twelfth-century poem, apparently from Shropshire, which appears to function as a hare charm. If a hunter, upon encountering a hare, is to have any luck capturing him, instructs the poem, he must lay upon the ground with his weapon in his hand, and utter the following seventy-seven names for the animal. Thus will the hare's strength be 'put down', enabling him to be captured.

The poem is in Middle English, and the names of the hare, most of them insulting, are captivating in this older version of our language. *Scotewine, babbart, wodecat, westlokere, wint-swifft, wortcroppere, gobigrounde, deuhoppere.* The modern English version is equally entertaining. Old big bum, fellow in the dew, cat of the wood, hedge frisker, swift-as-wind, squatter in the hedge, covenant breaker, stag with the leathery horns. *Old Goibert* is my particular favourite. I have no notion of the origin of this word, nor its precise meaning, but it is rather beautiful. Old Goibert. It sounds like an invocation.

One name missing is that given to us by Bede four centuries before: the name of a supposed Anglo-Saxon goddess whose memory lingers in the modern Easter, and which is regularly ritually abused by hordes of ridiculous modern so-called Druids and Pagans wandering about on the downs, polluting the circles and barrows with their incense sticks and magic crystals. I suppose I should be more charitable to these people. They are lost like everyone else. At least it gets them out of the house. But why is it necessary to dress up like vampires?

In *Temporum Ratione*, Bede tells us that April was known to the Anglo-Saxons as *Eosturmonath*, for this reason: *Eosturmonath has a name which is now translated 'Paschal month', and which was once called after a goddess of theirs named Eostre, in whose honour feasts were celebrated in that month.*

Hence the modern Easter. But this supposed goddess, Eostre, appears in no other source. Why not? Bede is unlikely to have invented her. Perhaps she was a localised deity. There are other such in Bede's writings – Erce, for example, possibly a goddess of the Earth, who is found nowhere outside his work. Bede is good at rooting out old pagan customs, I think. He is fascinated by them, even as he seeks to bury them with his own religion. If Eostre ever existed, Bede would find her.

As for the hare – well, moon goddesses, Earth goddesses, hare goddesses are often tied up together. Eostre's month is the time when hares mate, box, leap in the fields. The Easter Bunny is a memory of the old hare goddess, shrunk down to fit the withered glare of modernity, tied up in ribbons for children. I can prove nothing. But several old English rural tales tell of hares being born from eggs. This may be because hares nest in fields, where ground-nesting birds laid their eggs before the coming of the tractors. Easter eggs, Easter rabbits. And then we hear of the one hare story that is common in old cultures all around the world: that the hare can transform at will into a woman; and a woman into a hare.

Who is it that dances up there?

at this, the fire flares and rises
the circle draws back
moon's eye is now wide and full above us
the flames cycle through colours
orange to red

purple
white
the fire is white and high
we step back further
in the flames now, a shape moves
our music falls silent

we wait

The saddest story from Imber is that of Albert Nash. Albert was the village's last blacksmith. From the old pictures it is possible to see how close-knit this village was. It is possible to see how little must have changed since the hare charm was written in Middle English. Scarcely more than a hundred and fifty people, living up on the high plain. A blacksmith, an inn, the old windmill. Granny Staples' old shop. Jabez Early, maker of dew ponds. The Deans at Seagram's farm. And Albert. When the villagers were ordered to evacuate, Albert was found weeping, it is said, over his anvil. Of all the people of Imber, he found it hardest to break his ties with the land his family had lived on since before any recorded memory.

Albert lived less than six months after his exile. A strange thing happened. I can prove nothing. But it is said that his wife, Martha, awoke one night to find him dressed and pacing the bedroom. He wore his boots, as if he had been outside; they were wet with dew. The moon was full; I would place money on this, though I can prove nothing. Albert paced the boards, wide-eyed. He had seen something, I think. He had been out, and seen something. Martha asked him what he was doing. Albert said only: *I am going home.*

Martha persuaded him to undress and return to bed. When she awoke the next morning, she found Albert dead beside her.

from the fire then she comes
the White Lady
she stands before us
all in the circle fall to our knees
flames white
stones white
moon white
She stands before us
none dare look at her face

we bow our heads

Hare-women are not always goddesses, of course, and they are not always benevolent. I know of no god or goddess who is always benevolent. But in any case, many of the old suspicions that surrounded the hare in British folk culture seem to come from her association with the witch. There is a variant on a single story which is found in dozens of places across these islands. A hunter is out with his dogs when they encounter a hare. The dogs give chase and manage to injure the animal, biting it on the leg or pulling off a piece of its fur, but the hare escapes. The next day the old woman of the village, long suspected of witchcraft, is nursing an injury in the same place the hare was bitten.

There is the negative aspect of these small, isolated villages in one common tale. God protect the old woman who made too many enemies. Nobody can ever quite be trusted. I have learnt this in my long life. There is a darkness about this world.

It is wiser to live alone. Stay silent, walk with your head down. Speak only when spoken to. That way, many of life's arrows may miss you, if you are lucky.

I cannot say I have really been lucky. But it was a long time ago. Most things were a long time ago now. This is one of the few benefits of advanced age.

my head still lowered
I stand as others kneel
I speak

White Lady, I say,
bless us
bless our people
bless our land
bless this sanctuary
accept in exchange
our offering

there is silence
and then there is movement
a wind blows from the west

we wait

when we look up, She is gone

I have been preparing for a long time. For all of these years, I suppose, I have been preparing. Since I first came across the story of the dancing hare, since my interest became what some might call an obsession. I would prefer to call it a preoccupation. I don't know how many years it has been now. Does it matter?

I have been looking for her before, of course. Casual trips at first, up on to the downs. Visits to Imber, when the public was allowed. But it's no good just wandering about. There are calculations to be made. There is serious research to be done. She will not simply reveal herself to any casual passer-by. It has been necessary to track down and consult all the published tales and square them with the old maps, in order to effectively calculate where these events occurred. It has been necessary also, as far as has been possible, to align the stories with the dates, and even times, of the incidents. It has been complex and time-consuming. But time is something I have at my disposal, for now. And it has been enjoyable. I will miss it, I think.

But it is done now. I have identified a relatively small area, between the henge and the village, where I believe the sightings to have occurred over a period of several centuries. They have all occurred, as best I can see, under a full March moon – the hare moon, to use its folk name – at dusk.

It is a hare moon tonight.

I am waiting for dusk now. Up here, it creeps in across the hills like some being. I have chosen a site within my prescribed area. A standing stone, long fallen on its side, on the long shoulder of the plain. The view to all sides is beautiful. Imber is hidden beneath the brow of the next hill. Skylarks call as dusk approaches.

Date, time and place: I am as close, I believe, as anyone could ever be. But there is one variable I cannot control. She appears to those who need her. That much is certain. She offers something to them. It is clear enough from the tales that nobody expects or asks for what she brings. I suppose you could sit here through a hundred moons and never see a thing. She decides. She knows what you need.

The moon is rising now above the plain. The night is purple.

I am determined not to hunt. I am not a hunter. I did not bring binoculars, a camera, a notebook. None of that. I will sit on this stone with my hip flask, I will warm my body as the night grows cold.

What will be will be.

And then, suddenly, it is. I almost do not turn my head. It is impossible, really, that this should be anything more than a way to pass my time at this late stage in my life. Impossible that my games in the library and museum could come to anything.

But there she sits. In front of me and to my left, perhaps twenty yards away. A hare.

The evening is darkening as she begins to move to my right. She is a big one. The tips of her ears are coal black, her eyes saucer-like. She completes the first circle around me as I sit on the stone. I dare not move. She circles again. Faster this time. And again. Now her feet begin to thump on the ground. Her back feet push up, her rear end rises, now she rolls, as if somersaulting, faster, still faster, and now I can sit no longer, I raise myself up, I turn with her dance, I follow her as the night comes in and the moon brightens. The hare runs, faster still, faster than I have ever seen a hare run, she leaps, jumps, yes, she dances. She dances, and she keeps dancing as the night comes down and then she is dancing no longer, then she is standing before me and it is not a hare now.

It is not a hare now.

She approaches.

I did not realise how heavy my heart was. I did not realise the weight I carried. All of these years. I had thought the weight was the world and everything in it, but it was the weight of my heart.

It has been so heavy.

She stands before me now. I dare not look. Somehow I find myself kneeling. The moon silvers the grass of the plain as if it were day beyond the veil.

It is lighter now.

It is much lighter now.

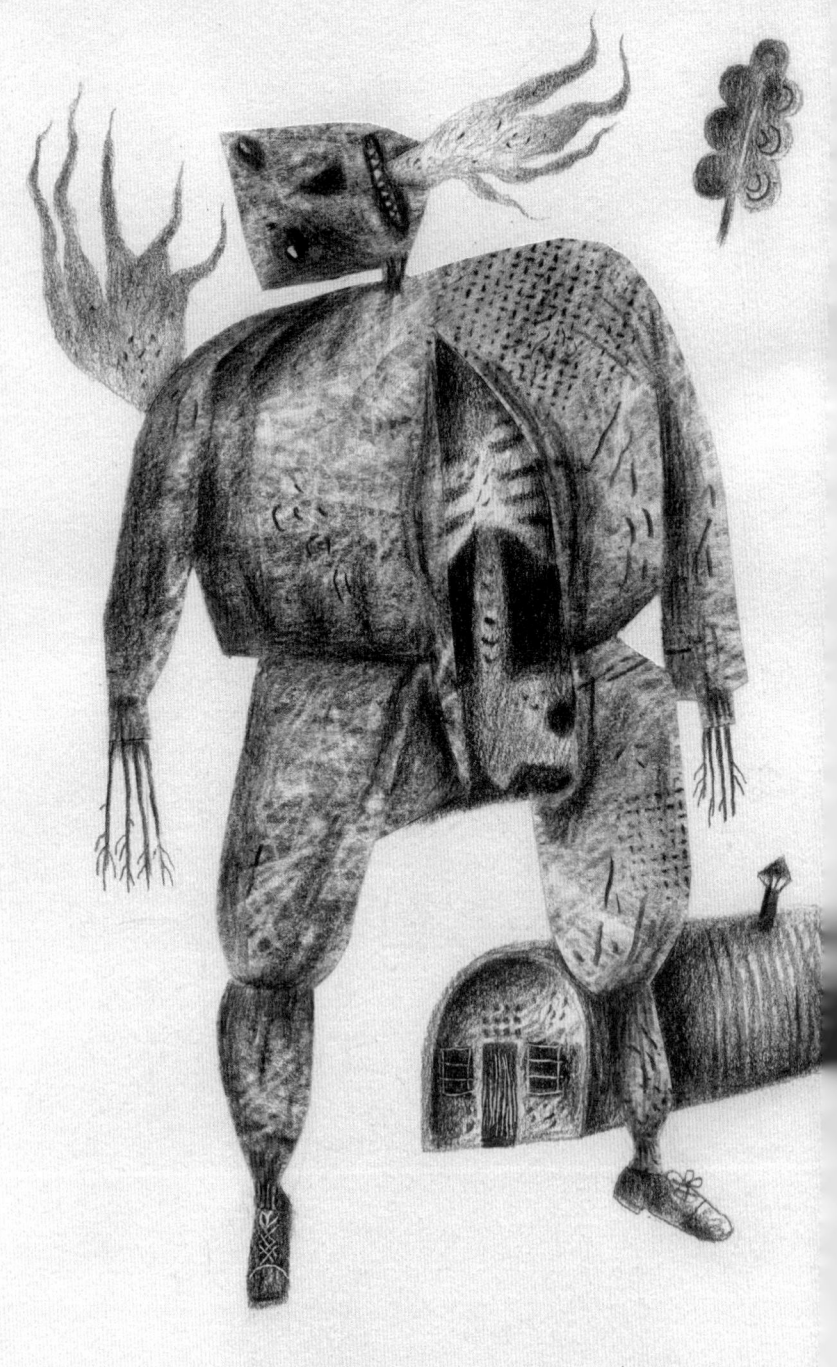

The Hand
Under
the Stone

Sarah Hall

NOBODY BELIEVES YOU when you talk about the whispering. *Oh, Monny, you are funny*, they say, *you've such an imagination*. There's a lot they don't believe. Like when you say the river has very old creatures living in it, with great long jaw-bones and rainbow skin. You've seen them swim downstream between the weeds, not just during the fever when you had German measles, but other times. Or that one of your elbows, the one that got broken falling off the back of TJ's bike, knows about rain: when it will rain, when it will stop raining. Twinge-twinge ache. Or that something in the garth near the Nissen hut, where TJ has his bonfires, is rotten and wrong and makes you feel ill.

When you tell them about the tall stone whispering, they roll their eyes, or laugh, and won't even play it as a game. Mum. Bethany and Florence. Even Aunty Ro, who has mermaid hair and smokes relaxing cigarettes, and who has taken you on a few trips round the county to see the other circles and henges, doesn't believe. She smirks and nods. *Wow*, she says. *Amazing. You're very sensitive, Monny*. Aunty Ro's boyfriend Ed tuts and shakes his head. *Not surprised this one's starting to fray too*. It's ok. Sometimes it's better to not know when something is true. People, including grown-ups, spend a lot of time pretending, to make life easier. TJ's the only one who might have taken you seriously. He takes everything seriously. But you can't tell him anything now.

It isn't a lie. If you walk round the circle twice, touching each stone and counting, and if it's the same number both times, when you put your ear against the tallest, witchy looking one that stands to the side of the group, she whispers. You're good at numbers. Your teacher, Mrs Callahan, always says so. Not so good at concentrating in assembly, eating your lunch, especially mince, or writing not mirror-way. A-C-I-N-O-M. You can go up to a thousand, no problem, more if you want, though it gets boring, like a road that goes on and on and on. The biggest number doesn't exist anyway.

In the circle, which is more like a big squashed egg, there are less than a hundred stones. You know who they are. Each stone is like a person. Each has bumps, smooth bits, scrapes and chips; each has mountain-copied shapes, like the Castlerigg stones, flat-topped, saddle-backed, peaky; each is booming over or is still upright, has beardy moss or sparkle crystals inside. You know them like you know your friends and relatives, all the people in the village.

Apart from the farm and the Hall, yours is the closest house to the circle. The cottage belongs to the estate, where your dad used to work before he went, and your mum's got a lifelong contract to rent it very cheap. Some kind of old tenant's right that Ed says is *rarer than hen's teeth*. Ed and Aunty Ro live in a bungalow on the Carleton estate in town. TJ has built his own home out of the metal Nissen hut in the garden. It's got wooden extensions, an underground dugout entrance as well as the proper door, and it has a line off the cottage's electricity supply. There were complaints when everyone realized he was actually living there, to your mum, then to the estate, then to the council. Ed says all the time that TJ's hut looks like *shantytown* and is an *eyesore*. But it's been a few years now, and people have got used to it.

You can see the tall stone from your bedroom. The cottage radiators run on oil and the window streams with condensation, which is made of your breaths, in the mornings. When you've wiped it, you can see the top of her. And when the sky behind is stark blue, you can see the vee cut into the head of sandstone. She's very, very old. In school, Mrs Callahan talked about the people who made the megaliths in Britain, thousands of years ago. She showed the class pictures of humans that were smaller, hairier, had axes, and lived in mossy huts quite like TJ's. How they fetched the stones and built them and why and what they did there is a mystery, Mrs Callahan said. She showed you pictures of Rollright, Avebury and Stonehenge. Then the class talked about their magical stories, about kings and warriors, goblins and dancing ladies, which, when you think about your own village's circle, seem truer somehow.

The tall stone is warm, even in winter. When you put your hands on her she doesn't feel chilly like the others. It's as if she's not quite gone out, like TJ's bonfires the day after. She's reddish and has spirals on one side. Mrs Callahan brought the class over from school to look and you were all supposed to make tracing paper rubs of the spiral patterns. That was upsetting, everyone touching her. You stood to the side and wouldn't do it, even though Miss Cat, the teaching assistant, said, *come on, Monica, join in*.

The other stones are the tall one's daughters. They can't all have been daughters really, if once upon a time she was a human, because there are far too many. They're grey and white, like the rock all around the valley. Thicker. Colder. It's obvious she is the special one. She stands outside the circle, like a leader – a person in charge. She's probably the size of eight of you, standing on the shoulders of each other. About halfway up, she starts to lean over, like she's bending down listening to someone smaller, and when you stand underneath it makes you feel safe. It was Aunty Ro who first told you about what happened. She was once a village woman with tremendous powers. She could speak to the wind and heal people and help them have babies and stop rain spoiling people's vegetables. She was dancing on the moor. Other women, the daughters, were all dancing too. They were having a party and not going to church. A wizard who also believed in God saw them and was so angry that he put a spell on them. Their fingers and toes went stiff. Their arms and legs and eyes became hard. They froze. Aunty Ro said that's the way it is for women. They're stopped. It seems like a common story that some of the other circles have it too. Powerful, dangerous people: turned to stone.

In December, a few days before Christmas, Aunty Ro goes and leaves bits and bobs beside the tall stone. Tomatoes from the Co-op and bags of sage. Two oak trees have been planted inside the circle and Aunty Ro ties red ribbons on the low branches. Lots of people do it. They come in vans and camp along the road by the cottage garth. Ed thinks it's ridiculous. *Shag-vans*, he calls them. The circle-worshippers make little fires on the moorside and sometimes, if it hasn't rained for a long time, they accidentally set fire to the gorse. TJ hates that. The last time it happened he came running out of the hut and banged on the sides of the vans. *Fucking hippies*, he shouted, *fuck off back to where you came from. I'm the one who makes the fires!* I'm the one who makes the fires! Your mum ran out and apologized to them. She's good at calming things down, but it doesn't always work. If TJ is out of the hut, it means he's angry enough to not care about anything.

The circle-worshippers never want to fight anyway. They wear big velvet cloaks and purple dresses or leather trousers. Some of the women have bare boobs, even if it's frosty or raining. The things they leave against the stones are odd and quite grotty. Babies-in-tummies photos, where the babies look like submarines or moon-heads, tampons, rabbit tails, bundles of feathers, sticks and string made into dollies. They often try counting the stones too – you've seen them – but they never concentrate, or believe. They're like people reading the weather forecast rather than people getting wet or blown around. You could tell them: it's like unlocking a lock. The key has to be exactly right, not one missing bit or an extra tooth. They don't really expect the tall stone to speak or the daughters to be released. They're waiting for 3 o clock, when the sun sinks in her vee, so they can go and do what they do in their vans.

There's a secret. A hidden, underground stone. You know where it is, in the far bank near the farm, not really part of the circle anymore. One day it occurred to you it would be there, like a memory, and you dug down with a stick through the spiny grass and pebbles and roots and earth. It took a long time, but your mum was asleep after work and you were bored. After a while the stick started to scrape against something. You cleared a big gap and shovelled out the soil with your hands. There it was: pale as bone, with a waterhole in its surface like an eye looking up at you. There was such a strange feeling coming off it, shuddery, like an echo, and a smell too, like coal, or fireworks.

So, it's sixty-eight altogether, not sixty-seven. You thought about leaving the hidden stone uncovered, but didn't, because that was the first time you tried the count and got it right and the tall one whispered. All she said was, *no, don't show them*. So you shoved the earth back over the lost daughter. You went home with your nails black and grazes on your knuckles, and even though you could hear your mum talking about TJ on the phone to Aunty Ro, sounding as upset and worried, as usual, you felt really, really happy.

When you count the stones, you reach down and pat the bank too. You try to do it in a way that seems you're not doing it, like checking a shoelace is tied, in case anyone sees. After sixty-eight, clockwise, and sixty-eight backwards, you put your ear against one of the carved spirals, where it fits really well. You close your eyes and wait. It might be seconds or a minute or even longer. Sometimes there's nothing, just blocked, shell-ear sounds. Sometimes there's a sigh, then she speaks. Her voice is soft and insidey, like thoughts.

It's a bit like your mum's voice, when she's handling TJ. Quiet, calm, gentle. You've seen her confront him, in the garth, or out on the moor. If he almost can't hear what she's saying, he has to concentrate on her, and stop bashing and throwing things. He has to come closer, which makes your head rush with panic, but your mum stands very still. It's part of taming wild things – trusting that they won't kick or kill. Your mum can't touch TJ, and she doesn't try, but when they're nearer together it's as if something gets remembered, from when he was a little boy and they loved each other. She calls him Trevor. He gets confused instead of angry. He starts to rub his head and arms and to wipe at his eyes. *It's gone now*, your mum will say. *It's gone.* All of a sudden the storm dies, and TJ will go back into the Nissen hut, or get on his bike and pedal away as hard as he can.

She's brave, your mum. Or maybe she's doing something dangerous that she shouldn't be too.

It's a big surprise when one day the tall stone whispers: *help him.* You know straight away who she means, because when she speaks your brother's face is in your head. You keep your ear against the spiral and wait in case there's something more. But the tall stone is silent. You go home wondering what she means. You go up to your bedroom to think. These days, you never really see TJ, especially not in summer when the garth grass is high as a jungle, his vegetables are ripe, and he doesn't really need anything. You don't go near the hut unless your mum asks you to leave a cup of tea and a plate of biscuits on the wood stump outside the door on your way to school. The hut is mostly quiet. Your brother stays up late and sleeps into the day as far as you can tell. Sometimes there's a radio playing, or gunfire and games on his computer, or some kind of horrible scratchy music. Mostly the tea's still there, full, with a white skin floating on top, when you come back from school, and the biscuits have been nabbed by birds or rained soggy.

The Nissen hut is being swallowed by bushes, trees, and ferns. The metal corrugation is covered in bright moss, vines and dark yellow lichen. It's like it almost doesn't remember it's metal. There are systems TJ has for securing the doors and windows. The dugout tunnel entrance is round the back, behind blockages of wooden panelling and trees, in a private area where he grows and makes and burns things.

You've not seen inside for a long time. Last time you saw, when TJ was sick from a deep cut on his leg and needed antibiotics, you went in with your mum and had a nosy. There was a stereo and the old television propped on a trestle table, the battered laptop that school had bought him, a cold box and a Calor gas heater. There was a manky rope hammock tied up from the roof and in it books and magazines were in tipping-over piles. On a wall shelf was a row of jam jars with yellowy water inside, going from light to dark. A school photograph of his old class was taped to the wall, and you knew that one of the girls in the middle row of red cardigans used to be his girlfriend. Samantha. Samantha Fay. Her dad is headmaster at the secondary school in town. TJ had fitted a tiny log burner with a smoky black chimney. There were some boards over the earth floor. The old crocheted blanket from his bedroom was on a mattress, faded and dirty, and it was this blanket that made you feel saddest. The whole place was like a den – better, because it was properly fixed, and worse, because it was actually his home. It smelled like socks and mushroom soup and oil.

When your brother first took over the hut your mum was able to go and get his washing now and then. Your old dog Barns would go and sniff and scratch at the door and was sometimes let in. Sometimes you were let in too, just for a minute, if you didn't ask many questions or touch anything. The garth hadn't been barricaded up yet, and you could see what TJ was doing with the rainwater barrel, or when he was hammering structures and roping things. When he was building bonfires or cooking fish from the river. On really cold nights he might come back into the cottage for a few hours and sleep curled up on the sofa in front of the fire. He might pinch some milk from the kitchen in the morning, and talk to you a little bit, about his ideas, how the world was wrong, wars that had happened in the past and that would happen in the future, which was all fairly scary but interesting. Or he might leave a note of things he needed your mum to get for him. Phillips-head screwdriver, paraffin, extension cable. Other things he asked your mum for, she didn't get, and she would tut and sigh and put his notes in the bin. For a while, he was almost like part of the family, half moved out, but still like the TJ who used to bike you around and give you his old Lego, swing you between his legs, and babysit when your mum and dad went out to the pub.

Not anymore. He isn't coming back inside the cottage probably ever. Weeks go by with no sign of him. If you catch sight of him skulking between trees or on the road he looks much older than eighteen. He looks lean and sly as a pack-hound. A few times people have tried to sort him out. *An intervention*, Ed called it one time. He tried having a man-to-man chat out in the garden, telling TJ he should take his exams, or get a job and contribute, or move out properly. *You've got to be better than your dad, wherever he bloody is. Everyone has to help with the lifting – everyone should put their hands under the stone, son. You're acting like a mad prince out here.* TJ got very angry, told Ed he was a *cunt*, and slammed the door of the hut. Your mum had been standing awkwardly by the cottage and she asked Ed to leave. *Fine*, said Ed, *but he's taking advantage of you, Chrissy, and it's only going to get worse.* Your mum smiled tightly. *You don't understand the arrangement, Edward.* There were loud thumps from the back of the Nissen, like TJ was hurling bricks at the wall. You've tried before too. When Barns died of tummy cancer you stuck an invitation to the funeral you were having on the hut door. TJ didn't come.

You know he goes out at night though, because his bike is sometimes chained up in a new place in the morning. What he does, where he goes, you've no idea. Scavenging maybe. Looking for lumber or rooting in local skips. No one talks about him much in the village, at least not when you're there, or when your mum's there. Probably they don't want to hurt your mum's feelings. *Lost*, is what you've overheard them say. *He's a lost one*, even though everyone knows exactly where he is. At school sometimes they say stupid things about survivor TJ or psycho Trev. You heard Florence trying to explain it to the new girl, Lorin. Florence was slouching about like a gorilla with her jaw slack and her eyes crossed, then she pointed at you. *Her bog-eyed crazy brother*. Either Lorin didn't understand or didn't care, because she walked away and sat on the carpet ready for the register.

Deep down, they're scared. They're scared of the idea of him, a big wild boy living in a shed, and sometimes you even feel a bit proud. He's much older than your friends' brothers and sisters and much more unusual. Mostly you try to feel nothing. Dead-heart. Dead-head. Then it can't bother you. The fact he turned into a bogeyman who started shouting at you too. *Piss off, Monny, just piss off, you little bloody bint.* You don't talk about it with your mum, and she only talks about it when she has to. Like after the council was called by a neighbour complaining about planning permission. Or when the social worker was coming. When she tells you to get your coat and bag for school and take out the tea and biscuits. *Leave this for your brother on your way*, she says. Like it's a normal thing to do. Saucer of sugar-water for the bees, bucket of vegetable peels for the hens, plate of digestives for Trevor.

But the tall stone has powers and she's always serious. You know that. So the next time your mum asks you to take over the tea, you don't scoot off straight away. You put the mug down on the stump, take a breath, and knock very softly on the Nissen door. Bing-bing-bong. You don't really want him to hear. You wait. He doesn't answer, of course. You wait a little while longer and then knock louder – a bit too loud. The metal door dooms under your knuckles. There are rusty scabs all over it. Your heart is really going fast and there are little clicks in your throat, like a grasshopper on your tonsils. It's not even possible to imagine what TJ might say if he comes. But there's no sound inside.

You step back and count to ten, which seems a reasonable number. Chaffinches scrap and squabble in the lane. A tornado jet throttles overhead. The wind is starting to haw down from the hills, snapping the laundry on the line, and your achy elbow knows it's going to rain. You wait. He might be looking through the dirty blacked-out window at you. He might be quietly undoing the lock. There's mould and moss in the door seal. Maybe he's only using the underground passageway now or the back window. Maybe he's asleep or right at the other end of the garth hauling wood. You want to run away, but the tall stone's whisper is in your head. *Help him*. She only says important things. Like, *father's dead* or *show her the lump*. You're about to put your hand on the handle – not to open the door, you wouldn't dare go in without your brother saying so – just to feel. Then you notice what he's done. Pieces of broken glass have been glued all over it. Big clear shards. It looks beautiful and horrible, a kind of spiny, see-through, junk anemone. Why would he do that? Why would he, when a child could have put their hand there and cut it right down to the bone?

You know why. The same reason he tried to make the garth fence electric and asked your mum for a hunting rifle and a ream of industrial pigeon spikes. The same reason he hangs dead animals up along the hut roof. Not rabbits and pheasants that could be eaten, but a cat, long and thin, its head busted open on the road. Or a hawk, stood dead in a perch on the top prong of the Nissen, its talons wired to hold it. He doesn't need Stay Out signs or an Alsatian. He's got his own mind. He's in his own world and has become someone else, crazy, careless. You look at the lethal door handle. And there's that feeling you try not to have anymore. An ache and no air, like after a punch in the chest. This is why it's better to not care either, to go rock-hard, so what your brother does doesn't hurt, even when he's not actually touching you.

You leave the tea and biscuit plate on the tree stump and walk away. Your eyes are prickling you can feel your mouth forking down. You walk halfway along the road towards the village. Then you turn and run back. You take the digestives off the plate and hurl them onto the moor as you walk to school, one by one, as hard and far as your arm can throw.

School's OK, most of the time. You can forget about home for a while. It's two-thirds of a mile from the cottage and you measure it on your step-watch. You're allowed to go by yourself now, but if the weather's bad your mum drives you in the Honda. The dinners all look the same, with melting cheese tops and chips or beans. The loos have wee all over the floor and by the end of the week the coats in the cloakroom next door sometimes smell of wee. The building backs onto the woods so deer look over the fence and nibble the vegetable garden the Year Threes grow. Afternoons when you're outside doing forest school and looking at frogs or leaves are the best.

In class there are only two boys and there are twelve girls – thirteen now Lorin has started. Mrs Callahan is new too. She came halfway through the year when Mrs Cole got sick. Your class is called Blackbirds. All classes have bird names. Jays, Doves, Blackbirds, Swallows. Owls are the oldest and wisest. After Owls you'll have to go to the other school in town – the one your brother used to go to. Hopefully they don't remember him. He stopped going when he was fifteen.

Mrs Callahan is nice. She wears bright coloured shoes or glittery boots. Today she notices your hot cheeks. *How are you, Monny? Did you run all the way? Pardon*, you say. She repeats the question. Then you say, *good morning, Mrs Callahan* and *no*. You put your water bottle in the box by the name trays and get the books out of your book bag. You sit in the library corner pretending to read. You can feel Mrs Callahan looking over. Probably she'll come and check on you in a minute. Earlier in the year she started doing The Nest with one of the other teachers. The Nest is a quiet little room near the headmaster's office where there's extra help for children having trouble learning or where bothering things can be talked about. *To help any fledglings not yet flying*, it says on the door. You went twice to talk about concentration problems and it was fine. You told her about the circle being near your house. You told her about the tall stone whispering, and that you'd been to Castlerigg and Swinside and Mayburgh, and even down to the Nine Ladies with Aunty Ro, and that you thought maybe all the stones could speak, if they used to be people, and maybe they could talk to each other. Like a kind of stone telephone. Mrs Callahan said she was glad you'd enjoyed learning about those places. She showed you a book of legends and in it there were more stories, about petrified knights and sleeping armies, spells that kept the stones from being freed. She said some things that made you feel better. She said that there was lots of pressure these days for children to seem special and different and that was because grown-ups have forgotten to have any imagination. Things that seem miraculous to grown-ups about children are actually just normal. You didn't talk about TJ and you don't know if Mrs Callahan knows about him or not. Probably she does.

You don't talk to Florence when she comes into class. She's wearing a new sequin T-shirt and she tries to show you how the pattern changes colour when you brush it with a hand. The rainbow goes from pink-red-orange to blue-green-purple. *Do you want to have a go?* The thought of touching sequins, of touching anything pointy and scratchy, makes you feel sick again. You shake your head. Florence goes to show Bethany. That's the way it works with the three of you. It's tricky. Someone is usually left out. Sometimes the left-out one is chosen by the other two, sometimes, like now, number one chooses to be not part of the three. How it will be for the rest of the day is often decided when one of you is picked by Mrs Callahan to take the register to Mr Benning's office and has to choose a register partner. You glance over. Florence is standing with her chest and tummy stuck out. Bethany brushes and brushes the T-shirt. So what, you think.

You go over to the table where Lorin is writing on her notebook cover. She is writing her name. There's a little pointy roof over the i, not a dot. You move to the empty chair beside her so your bum is half on and half off the seat. She looks up at you with dark eyes. *Hi*, you say. She doesn't say anything. Her hair is curly and black and tied with a piece of ribbon. She's wearing the lilac slippers that she changes into every morning. Mrs Callahan explained to the class before she started that Lorin might stay at the school a while or a long time or might have to leave again soon, but everyone should make her feel welcome as a Blackbird. Lorin looks down at her book again. Mrs Callahan claps everyone to come over to the carpet. She calls the register and chooses Bethany to take it to the office. Bethany chooses Florence to help her.

After school you decide to go back to the circle and ask the tall stone a question. On the way you pick up a good stick and whack the cow parsley along the roadside, which is frothing like milkshake. You whip the heads clean off the stalks. You can hear a tractor chugging in a nearby field. No one is around at the circle and shadows are beginning to stretch behind each pillar. You think about the smaller humans that lived in Britain long ago in turf-houses and huts, rolling and dragging and heaving up huge pieces of rock, making sun-clocks and doorways and dolmens. They did it all with their hands. You think about the magical stories, men and women changed, because something in them was different, and they wouldn't follow rules, because they upset people.

Rain is just starting – big splattery splots – but you don't get your coat out of your backpack. You can see the roof of the cottage, your bedroom window. Dark smoke is pouring up out of the garth – TJ's burning something again. You do the count clockwise, then backwards. You look up as the tall stone leans over you. It's the first time you've ever asked her something. Usually it's all one way; her words come trickling into you. You try to concentrate. Why? Why should you help your brother, when he's such a *bastard* to everyone? Thinking it makes you feel angry all over again.

You put your ear on the tall stone's spiral. You wait. Nothing. Just a hum and heartbeat inside your ear. You lift your head away. It's raining properly and her sandstone is dark red, like the rust on the Nissen hut, or old bracken. She has a stonier smell when she's wet. You know rain makes things smell more what they are. Like Barns' fur after he'd been swimming in the river. Like the grass and gorse on the moor. The tall stone isn't speaking, because she's stone, just stone, and you feel stupid and angry and exactly like a child.

You run back over the moor, between the daughters, and over the road to the cottage. Your mum's car isn't there, but you don't take the key out from under the pot, open the door and go inside to watch television. Instead, you walk over to the Nissen hut. You skirt along the nailed wooden barricades. Smoke from the bonfire billows up above the garth, in great, mushroomy wafts. Even though it's raining, you know it won't go out. TJ's put petrol on – there's that tang in your nose like off a garage floor. You've never liked his bonfires, with their nasty fumes, but also because of how important and strange they are.

You move quietly to the spot where the holly tree juts out

88

and prop your backpack against the trunk. It's the hardest tree to climb; the leaves are thick and stabby and you never get up it without scratches. But it's the only place where you can see properly into TJ's secret world. The lower branches are knotty, with foot-steppers and holds. Higher up the hard green leaves bunch together and you have to scrape through spiky tunnels. You used to think the leaves were shrinking in, but you're just getting bigger and the tree measures you. This time you snag your sleeve and it takes a while to unpick it. The leaves rake your scalp. You wriggle down a branch that looms over the garth and look through a gap in the green, trying to spy TJ.

You see him walking towards the fire. You see him, but it's more like seeing some awful thing that looks like him. He's not wearing clothes. His skin is dark and his arms and legs are thin and dirty as old elastic bands. There's a black patch of hair on his crotch but he moves too quickly to see anything inside. The hair on his head is long and matty, twisted over one shoulder. When he turns, his backside is almost not there, just a dark crack with hardly any meat either side. He squats down by the bonfire, crouches very still, and you aren't quite sure he's real. It's like the shock of seeing a big, rare animal, its muscle and fur.

The flames lift high. They crackle up through a table made of brick with a metal grill – a bigger version of where he used to barbecue trout. You can't see what he's burning on it. Joined-up sacks of something. A round lump slumps off one side of the grill and two long bits dangle the other side. The loose threads of hessian flare red. Smoke chugs up and out. Where the septic cut was on his leg, there's an ugly scar. Your mum wanted him to get stitches because it kept opening and filling with pus. In the end, Ed got pills from a friend without a prescription. Now it's a wide patch of grey-white, shiny and pitted, like a battle mark in an elephant's hide. Your brother doesn't move. He is so still he almost disappears into the background. You don't move either, scared that he'll see or hear. You're covered by thick, camouflaging leaves, a T-shirt and jeans, but you suddenly feel completely bare.

The rain comes down, pattering the leaves, dripping on you. Your hands ache from clutching the branch, you need the toilet now, and it's getting cold inside the shadows of the holly. After a while your brother crab steps over to a pile of wood and throws more logs on the fire. Sparks explode. He picks up a long stick and prods the heap on the grill. He pushes and stokes until it rolls and flops over, and then you can see it better, between the flames. The two long bits of sack are wearing boots. They're legs. And the lump the other side, spilling open and flaring as sawdust ignites, is a head. He's burning a dummy made to look like a man.

His filthy, naked body. His animal squat. The thing in the fire. It is so horrible you feel like screaming. The branch under you seems to sway, and you could tumble off, headfirst into the garth, into his lair. You cling tighter. Your brother looks up at the sky, at the clouds rolling off the hills. He stands slowly. He scratches his side hard as if there are fleas. No, he is not TJ. TJ used to ride you around on his bike, and play football. He used to have friends and a girlfriend and eat and do homework at the kitchen table. He was a boy. He walks away into the garth and disappears behind the tall grass.

You begin to shuffle quickly back through the spears of holly, desperately toeing the branches behind. You can feel a hundred scratches on your arms and neck, and on your bare back as your T-shirt rips open. You jump down, grab your backpack, and run into the cottage. You go quickly up the stairs to your bedroom as your mum calls, *that you, Monny*, and shut the door. You sit on the window seat, trying to get your breaths down and to calm your heart, trying not to picture him in your head. Your T-shirt is torn almost in half. There's a patchwork of red gashes on your arms.

Low cloud and mist and smoke gather over the moor. You

can't see the tall stone – she's disappeared. But what she said, or what you heard inside your mind, is impossible. You can't help your brother. He isn't your brother. The truth is he isn't even a person anymore. He's trapped in that terrible form, heartless, and nameless, and ruined. And you know that in none of the stories where people are changed, are they ever changed back again. The curse is really a curse on those left living.

The Dark Thread

Graeme Macrae Burnet

Extract from the journal of Bram Stoker

Whitby, August 12th 1890

THE SHADOW from which I thought I had unshackled myself
has returned. Whether this Horror is real or merely the handiwork of my imagination I cannot say. Nor can I say which of
these possibilities disturbs me more. While I cling to the hope
that this vision will prove to be no more than a symptom of the
fatigue from which I am suffering, I fear I may be on the cusp
of losing my reason. Late as it is, sleep will not come and if it
does, I dread that my dreams will be haunted by what I witnessed not half an hour ago.

Florence and I arrived in Whitby this late afternoon, wea-
ry but in good spirits after our train journey from London. My
dear wife has been chastising me for unduly exerting myself in
the service of Henry, but though she is correct as always, there
can have been no avoiding it. Although the weather was un-
seasonably grey and chilly, the sea air had something of the
restorative effect it always has on me. We dined in our rooms
here at Royal Crescent and talked of our plans for the coming
weeks. In my anxiety to precipitate a feeling of relaxation, I

over-indulged in the wine and port provided, but my efforts had not their intended effect. By the end of our repast I felt more agitated than ever. Florence retired and I set out to take the night air, hoping to provoke the narcotic effect of physical exhaustion.

The town was asleep and my only company as I ascended the steps to St Mary's church was a large stray dog which must for a while have mistaken me for its master. He followed me through the cemetery that sits atop the East Cliff, before abandoning me to roam like a dark spectre in the fields adjoining the great Abbey which stands guard over the town. I then walked some miles along the cliffs to Saltwick Bay and the Black Nab. The moon was swathed in a gauze of cloud, but afforded enough light to guide me. There was nothing but silver and grey and the slow turning of the sea. I passed not a soul on my hike and nor would I have expected to, for who but the disturbed would be abroad on the cliffs at such a time?

After an hour or so I turned to retrace my steps. The eastern gable of the ancient Abbey, devoid of any protection from the elements, thrust above the horizon like the craggy eminences of the Carpathians. As I drew closer the outcrops of the transept resembled a copse of tombstones. The rearward drift of the clouds made the whole appear to pulsate. I had succeeded, I thought, through the exertion of my trek to ease my mind somewhat, until as I approached the gable, at a distance of perhaps one hundred yards, a figure appeared framed in the central archway of the uppermost level of the Presbytery. I was at too great a distance to distinguish more than the silhouette, but I knew at once to whom – or what! – this form belonged. Even had I doubted the evidence of my sight, the creeping sensation on my neck and scalp provided the corroboration that this was none other than the Horror which had been so long dormant. I quickened my pace and directed my eyes towards the sea, as if by averting my gaze I might erase the vision. I was unable to resist the urge to look back, however. For a happy moment, I thought it gone. The archway now framed no more than sky, but then I spied him again, on the lower level. His profile, at this closer proximity, was unmistakeable; the narrow hips topped by wide shoulders, so that the whole formed a slim triangle tapering towards the feet. His hands were clasped across his chest, in a manner which might have seemed obsequious were it not so menacing. I must I confess that I broke into a run, giving no thought to the narrowness of the path and the sharp drop of the cliffs to my right. Such was my fright that to tumble to my death would at that moment have seemed relief. Breathless, I opened the gate into the churchyard of St Mary's and scrambled through the tombstones paying scant respect for those resting beneath. At a certain point I stumbled to my knees and remained on the ground for some moments recovering my breath. Perhaps it was the corporeal effect of the damp sod on my palms, but I began to feel my reason return to me. What I had seen was a product only of my fatigue and the surfeit of port I had imbibed. I shook my head to myself and forced a laugh. I resolved to sleep late the following day and avoid strong victuals. Then despite the darkness, I felt a shadow pass across me. The Ghoul – Satan's myrmidon or whatever he might be – was standing before me. I struggled to my feet and faced him. He stood swaying almost imperceptibly, like the branch of a tree in a light breeze. I felt the blood coagulate in my veins. I was close enough to see the wisps of his grey moustache framing his thin lips. His breath, which was quite rank, escaped his nostrils in a cloudy stream. He unclasped a hand and began to extend it towards me. His mouth opened. I did not linger to hear his speech, however, but raised my cane and struck out at his head. He must have stepped back with preternatural speed, for my blow met with naught but air. And then he was gone. Terrorised as I was, I had no inclination to search for him. I dashed down the rough steps that descend into the town and over the bridge traversing the harbour, this putting me in mind for a moment of Tam

O'Shanter pursued by his hags. I did not pause until I had regained the sanctuary of our rooms in the Crescent.

Despite my better judgement I have, since I arrived back, endeavoured to settle my nerves with two or three glasses of port, but my agitation is stubborn and I feel I shall not sleep before dawn. It is a fearful thing for a man to question his own sanity, but so I must. I feel – *feel quite definitely* – the Ghoul's presence in the room, and yet when I gaze into the glass I see only myself.

***

From the Whitby Gazette, *August 22nd 1890*

INQUEST into DEATH OF LUCY SWANTREE

The inquest into the death of Miss Lucy Swantree, a maid, 19, late of Haggersgate, Whitby, has been conducted at the Crown Hotel under the direction of the coroner, Mr George Buchannan. The body of Miss Swantree, it will be remembered, was discovered in the cemetery of St Mary's church on the morning of August 13th. The first witness at the inquest, Mr Alfred Tinley, sexton at St Mary's, described how he had discovered Miss Swantree slumped against a tombstone on the morning in question. Thinking she was asleep, he sought to rouse her by means of shaking her by the shoulder, but it was right away apparent that she was not sleeping but deceased. The second witness was:—J.M. Agar, a doctor of medicine residing and practising in Whitby. He deposed that he was called to the scene and immediately pronounced Miss Swantree dead. Her body having been removed to a nearby hostelry, Dr Agar made his examination and discovered a fracture to the left side of the skull which he concluded to be the cause of death. No other marks or injuries were recorded. In reply to the coroner, Dr Agar stated that it seemed most likely that Miss Swantree had lost her footing and struck her head on a gravestone causing the fatal injury. The third witness was:— Mina Caffyn, 18, also resident at Haggersgate. Miss Caffyn tearfully deposed that Miss Swantree had told her that she had arranged that evening to meet Mr Thomas Creaser, a cooper, whom she described as

Miss Swantree's fiancé. The fourth witness:—Mr Thomas Creaser deposed that he had indeed arranged to meet Miss Swantree on the evening in question, but had not done so. He further denied that he had ever been betrothed to Miss Swantree or given her cause to believe this to be the case. He stated that he had been drinking all evening in the Black Horse Inn and had stayed the night there. This evidence was corroborated by the fifth and sixth witnesses:—Mr Harold Edley, landlord at the Black Horse Inn, and Mr William Ackroyd, a friend of Mr Creaser. The final witness was:—Inspector Hugh Sorsby. Inspector Sorsby deposed that he attended the examination of Miss Swantree's body carried out by Dr Agar. He later made an inspection of the churchyard and found nothing to suggest that foul play had occurred.

This being the whole of the evidence, the jury (Mr R. Lennard, foreman) returned the following verdict: that the deceased died of a blow to the head following a fall. Mr Buchannan then concluded proceedings.

***

Extract from the police log of Inspector Hugh Sorsby,
August 14th 1890

Further to the discovery of the body of Miss Lucy Swantree, I had yesterday afternoon an interesting visitor, this in the person of a Mr Bram Stoker. Mr Stoker presented himself at the station, having explained that the landlady of his boarding house had told him of the tragic event in the churchyard of the previous evening. Mr Stoker let me to understand that he is a gentleman of some renown in the theatrical circles of London and having no reason to doubt him, I received him in my study and offered him a glass of port which he accepted. He was of impressive stature and dress, but exhibited a certain garrulousness and eagerness to please, which ill befitted his status. He first began by asking if there were any suspicious circumstances surrounding the death of the poor girl. I would not be drawn on this, and instead put it to him that if he had some information suggesting this to be the case he was obligated to share it. After some minutes of waffling, during which he twice rose from his seat and paced about the room, he told me that due to some agitation of the mind, he had taken a late evening walk along the cliffs towards Robin Hood's Bay. As his discourse was dreadfully long-winded and replete with unnecessary detail, I interjected to ask if he had seen Lucy Swantree. He answered in the negative, but instead told me that he had fleetingly observed a black-clad figure, first wandering among the ruins of the abbey and then in the churchyard at St Mary's. He was unable to furnish me with great detail, other than that he was a tall, slender gentleman of a certain age, dressed in a black frock coat and tight-fitting trousers. He could not say precisely what time he saw this gentleman, as he had not his pocket-watch upon him, but it must have been close to midnight. I thanked Mr Stoker for volunteering this information and wished him a pleasant stay in the town. This morning I made a tour of premises in the vicinity of St Mary's and enquired as to whether any of those residing there had seen either Mr Stoker or this mysterious dark figure. As the answers were all in the negative, the matter merited no further action.

***

Letter from Florence Stoker to Dr Andrew Billington, Harley Street, London, August 21ˢᵗ 1890

My dear Andrew,

I am fulfilling my promise to write to you about Bram's health. I have resisted the desire to write sooner (we have been now a week in Whitby), hoping that with the passing of time I might have better news. I regret to tell you, however, that the contrary is the case. Bram is more disturbed than ever. During the day, he has none of his usual energy and vivacity. He seems weighed down by a kind of languor. I fear that Mr Irving has drained all his reserves of energy and there is nothing left for his wife. In the evening he comes alive a little. He writes furiously in his journal (which I have dared not open for fear of confirming my anxieties about his state of mind) and demands not to be interrupted while doing so. Over dinner, he discourses volubly, but his thoughts are often disordered, and at times might be taken for no more than the ravings of a madman. He has become quite obsessed with an incident that occurred on the evening of our arrival here. A young girl was found dead from a fall in a churchyard. Bram propounds wild theories about the true cause of her death, while simultaneously holding that the police suspect that he is guilty of her murder and are only waiting for him to incriminate himself to tighten their noose. When I have persuaded him to leave our rooms, he looks constantly about him, believing that he is everywhere being followed.

These last two days have seen a worsening of his condition. He has quite turned day into night. Since our arrival, he has been unable to sleep and noisily paces our sitting room, muttering to himself. He comes abed only towards dawn and dozes fitfully for a few hours.

O Andrew, I fear the worst. I know that any suggestion of Bram visiting a doctor here in Whitby would be met with scorn (you know how pig-headed he can be), and in any case I fear that the physicians here in the provinces lack the wherewithal to deal with such a case. It would be too great an imposition to ask you to travel so far, but I plead for your advice and ask whether you might send some draught or tonic to subdue him. It remains my hope that if we may only break this cycle with some proper rest, our dear jolly Bram might be restored to us.

[Signed]
Florence

***

Letter from Dr Andrew Billington to Florence Stoker,
August 22nd 1890

Dear Florrie,

You must not vex yourself. The mostly likely explanation for the symptoms you describe in your husband is simply exhaustion. I do not doubt that some sleeping draught might ease his condition, but without examining him in person I am reluctant to send a prescription.

Your misgivings about my provincial colleagues are entirely without foundation. As it happens I know a local man for whom I can vouch without reservation. His name is Dr John Agar and he has a villa on the West Cliff. As well as being a first rate physician, he is a convivial and entertaining host. I have written to tell him to invite you to dinner, where I am sure you will spend a pleasant evening and he will have the opportunity to observe Bram without the formality of a consultation. I have no doubt that an evening in Dr Agar's company will in itself have a restorative effect.

With warmest wishes,
Andrew

***

Abraham (Bram) Stoker was born to a middle class family in Clontarf, a few miles north of Dublin, in 1847. He was a sickly child, unable to walk until he was seven. His mother Charlotte was a great storyteller and Bram was weaned on the Irish lore of banshees, fairies and the Dearg-due, the flame-haired bloodsucker who was said to tempt men with her beauty before drinking their blood. Young Bram found himself under the care of his Uncle William, a doctor specialising in bloodletting. The application of leeches was the then current treatment for childhood measles, and decades later Stoker would describe his most famous creation as 'like a filthy leech, exhausted with his repletion.'

Stoker's health recovered and he developed into an able athlete and student of sufficient calibre to enrol at Trinity College. He then joined the civil service, but it was his unsalaried role as theatre critic for the Dublin *Evening Mail* (at that time edited by Sheridan le Fanu, author of the famous vampire story *Carmilla*) that would lead to a life-changing meeting. Henry Irving was the leading actor of his day, and having read Stoker's review of his performance as Hamlet in 1876, he invited him to dine at his suite at the Shelbourne Hotel on St Stephen's Green. Two years later he appointed him manager of the Lyceum theatre in London which he had recently acquired. The pair became inseparable. They worked, dined, drank and toured together. Stoker was in Irving's thrall, but Irving depended on his manager for everything.

Stoker's energy was boundless. Despite the enormous demands placed on him by Irving, he still found time in 1878 to marry Florence Balcombe, a penniless but beautiful colonel's daughter from Falmouth. Later, perhaps hoping to step out of Irving's shadow, he began to write. Of his first novel, *The Snake's Pass*, an Irish-set tale of lost treasure, Stoker's biographer Barbara Belford concludes that, 'his writing habits ... were always better suited to the short story.' Of a later novel, *The Athenaeum* gloomily pronounced that 'the book bears the stamp of being roughly and carelessly put together ... the less said about *The Shoulder of Shasta* the better for everyone concerned.' There is, of course, only one work for which he is remembered. *Dracula* was certainly not roughly and carelessly put together. Stoker completed it in the Kilmarnock Arms hotel in Cruden Bay in 1897, but the idea had been gestating for seven years, if not since he heard the story of the Dearg-due at his mother's knee. And despite his wide travels, it was the sleepy port of Whitby that he chose for the Count to affect his entry into England.

***

Extract from the journal of Bram Stoker

Whitby, August 24th 1890

We spent this evening in the company of Dr John Agar, who has a villa on the West Cliff only a short walk from here. I have not been in a sociable frame of mind, but Florence persuaded me, and I'm glad that I acquiesced.

The evening began with a glass of port in Dr Agar's library. His large collection of books included not only the usual works of history, poetry and romance, but also a considerable number of works devoted to folklore and the occult. He took us on a tour of the room, pausing now and then to slide a volume from the shelf and pass it to me to peruse. His eagerness spoke, I thought, of the want of sophisticated society that those who live in provinces must suffer. Florence, in her charming manner, drew us away from the shelves and the conversation in which we had become absorbed. He turned his attention all to her, as men are wont to do, and patiently answered her enquiries. He has led a fascinating life, serving as ship's doctor on voyages to every corner of the globe, as well as spending some years as chief surgeon in the Asylum at Caterham. Despite being in his fifties, he has never married. 'Some men,' he said with a hint of sadness, 'are simply not made for such things.' When Florence asked why he had settled in Whitby he deflected the question by asking instead what had drawn us here. Before either of us had the chance to answer, a housekeeper entered and informed us that dinner would be served. We then removed to a panelled salon decorated by paintings and artefacts accumulated on Dr Agar's travels. A great fire roared in the hearth.

Dr Agar was a generous host and our glasses were never permitted to empty. So diverting was his conversation that I barely noticed the dishes we were served, but I am certain I ate with an appetite that has been lacking in recent days. It was only when the meal was over, and our tongues had been loosened by wine that our talk returned to the subject of our present domicile. Whitby, Dr Agar informed us, was a very singular town. 'There is,' he said, 'a dark thread running through the history of this place.' He then glanced towards Florence and said that some topics were not suitable for such congenial company. Florence assured him that there was no subject that need be debarred from her ears, but nevertheless insisted that, due to the hour, we must presume on his hospitality no further. Dr Agar nodded his assent. He then, under the pretext of showing her a painting, drew Florence away, while I warmed my buttocks at the fire and finished the cigar I was smoking. When he returned he pressed a number of volumes into my hands, promising that he was sure they would be of interest to me, and with that we made our departure. It was long past midnight when we stepped out. The sky was clear and the waning moon was a crisp crescent, unfettered by clouds. Florence remarked on how fortunate we had been to make Dr Agar's acquaintance and I heartily agreed. Across the harbour the silhouette of the Abbey stood sentry over the town, but I averted my eyes from it, to thus eschew any unsolicited visions. The streets were silent, other than for the distant yowling of a hound. As we walked the short distance to Royal Crescent, however, I sensed that we were not alone and felt the familiar creeping sensation on my scalp. For fear of alarming Florence I neither gave voice to my feeling, nor so much as glanced over my shoulder. Instead I remarked on the chill of the night air and quickened our pace so that we might we regain our rooms with alacrity.

I had thought to look over the volumes which the good doctor has so kindly lent me, but a great torpor has come over me. I must lay down my pen and welcome it, as sleep has not come easily to me these last days.

***

Dearest Andrew,

I cannot think how to repay you. Yesterday we were welcomed into the home of Dr Agar, and a kindlier, more fascinating gentleman we could not wished to have met. We spent the evening in most stimulating conversation, with no hint of our true purpose. Before we took our leave, he found a pretext to draw me away to another room, where he gave me his impressions. Bram, he said, was unquestionably in a restive state of mind (over dinner he had frequently interjected with bizarre remarks, made *a propos* of nothing), but the doctor was of the opinion that exercise and a general avoidance of sensation and excitement would prove adequate remedy. He gave me a powder which I could administer without Bram's knowledge, and this I did on our return to our rooms. Bram is now sleeping with a tranquillity that he has not known since we arrived here. I am so greatly reassured. I know that you would not wish any recompense for this service you have done me, but please know, dear Andrew, that I am in your debt.

> With deepest gratitude,
> Florence

***

Extract from the journal of Bram Stoker

Whitby, August 25ᵗʰ 1890

I awoke this morning feeling quite restored in energy and humour. For the first time in many weeks, my sleep was undisturbed by unwelcome visions. Such was the depth of my slumber that I missed breakfast. What a fine fellow John Agar is to have produced this effect. And what captivating company he is. I must renew my acquaintance with him at the earliest opportunity. This afternoon Florence and I took a walk along the sands to Runswick, where we took some simple fare at an Inn, surrounded by fishermen with hands and faces as gnarled as driftwood. Their talk was all of the sea and those it has taken. Florence was in good spirits, which pleased me as she has lately been in uncharacteristically melancholy humour. She confessed that she has been concerned about my health and seemed relieved when I admitted that I had not felt quite myself. We discussed our evening with Dr Agar and agreed that we had been fortunate to find such congenial society in a backwater like Whitby. It was only then, as we looked out across the bay, that I recalled the phrase he had used at the conclusion of the evening.

[...]

Later

I have begun I believe to unravel the dark thread of which Dr Agar spoke. Like the loose thread of a hem, one cannot help but tug at it, irrespective that in so doing one may destroy the garment. Florence and I dined at home in companionable silence, fatigued after our trek along the sands. Afterwards, she kissed me on the forehead and made me promise not to be long in following her to bed.

I turned to the books Dr Agar had lent me. The weightiest of these was *The History of Whitby and of Whitby Abbey* by Lionel Charlton, dating from 1777. As I turned the pages I discovered that certain passages in this and the other volumes had been annotated by Dr Agar or some previous owner. I shall here summarise my findings, in the hope that in committing them to paper I might expose the fallacy of the disturbing conclusions to which they point.

The great Abbey of Whitby was established in the seventh century by St Hild, a nun who – in a similar way to our own St Patrick – is said to have driven the snakes which infested the surrounding area from the very cliffs along which I had walked on my first evening here. St Hild was herself bitten by an adder, but she was inexplicably unharmed, save for two small lumps on her arm. Local superstition has it that this driving away of the snakes manifested itself in the frequency of the coiled ammonites found on the cliffs and shores here and sold as charms to ward off evil.

By the twelfth century a ritual termed the Penny Hedge ceremony had arisen in these parts. On the eve of Ascension Day, townspeople cut wooden stakes and erect a fence along the shoreline, shouting Out on ye, Out on ye. The origins of this tradition are said to lie in the accidental killing of a hermit-monk by huntsmen, after a boar they were pursuing ran into his hut in the vicinity of the Abbey. This implausible story is dismissed by Mr Charlton as no more than 'a fiction', but if one construes that this killing was neither accidental nor that its victim was an innocent monk, but was instead a more sinister type of being, it requires no great leap of the imagination to see why it might have given rise to a ritual involving the cutting and driving of wooden stakes.

The thread continues. In the thirteenth century a man called Thomas Chaloner discovered the cliffs of Whitby to be rich not only in ammonites but also in Alum, a valuable commodity in the production of dyes and curing of leather. At that time, the Pope held a monopoly over the trade in Alum, and Chaloner, not having the competence to manufacture it himself, travelled to Italy and induced two of the Pope's men to travel in secret with him to England to set up an Alum works. These men, it is written, were transported in casks, but the subterfuge was discovered and the Pope issued a curse on the three of such ferocity and length that a portion of it is worth recording here:

May they be cursed in living and in dying, in eating and in drinking, in being hungry and in being thirsty, in fasting and in sleeping, in slumbering and in waking, in walking and in standing, in sitting and in lying, in working and in resting, in pissing and in shitting, in sweating and in blood-letting. May the Son of the living God, with all the glory of his majesty, curse them; and may heaven, with all the powers which move therein, rise up against them to damn them, unless they shall repent, and make proper satisfaction for this their crime.

While I cannot speak to the importance of the Alum industry to the Pope's empire, his fury at this loss of two mere artisans seems wildly excessive. The cause of his great ire goes unmentioned in the curse, but two details lead me to believe that Chaloner's plot involved something more sinister than the manufacture of Alum: first, the men were said to be transported in casks – there is but one creature which, requiring the sustenance of the soil of its native land, would necessitate such an extraordinary means of conveyance. And, second, that the Pope is moved to curse them in their 'blood-letting'. Could there be a clearer indication of the true nature of these alleged artisans?

Having tugged at this thread, I cannot fail to reach the conclusion that this tranquil place is no less than a portal; a gateway to these islands for those shape-shifting blood-suckers designated around the globe as Strigoi, Estries, Jiangshi or Vampyres.

It then struck me quite forcibly that it was not the creature I encountered at the Abbey that had followed me here, but *I* that had followed *him*. And that, furthermore, it was conceivable that it was not he that was my shadow, but *I* that was *his*.

***

Letter from Florence Stoker to Dr Andrew Billington,
August 26ᵗʰ 1890

Dear Andrew,

I write in great distress. Bram, I fear, has quite lost his senses. He was awake all night with some books lent to him by Dr Agar, and this morning has been raving unintelligibly about adders, ammonites and various creatures of the night. Of course, I do not know the medical terms, but he seems to be not in possession of his reason. I ran at first to Dr Agar's villa, but despite my pleas, his housekeeper insisted that he was asleep and could on no account be disturbed. Not knowing where else to turn, I have packed up our belongings and had them sent to the station. We shall return to London this very night. I fear this place has had a most unnatural effect on Bram's state of mind and can only hope that the leaving of it will restore him to me.

I beg that you might find time to call on us at the earliest opportunity.

Yours,
Florence

***

Extract from the journal of Bram Stoker

Whitby, August 26ᵗʰ 1890

When I set down my pen last night, I had no thought for sleep. I set out first for the harbour and then through the narrow streets which lead to the steps of St Mary's. Knowledge is the enemy of fear, and the insight I had gained had dissipated the terror I felt on my first evening here. I walked briskly, like a man unburdened, but as I approached the steps the old creeping sensation came over me once more. My scalp tingled and a current ran down my spine. I felt a weakening in my legs which brought to mind the paralysis that afflicted the first years of my existence on this planet. My mind was unaffected, however. My plan was to seek out the Devilish creature and through confronting him, somehow make myself his master. I passed the Black Horse Inn, where I had once or twice taken an ale and listened to the stories of the locals, and the little shops selling Whitby jet and ammonites to tourists. All was silent. The clock on the church tower showed three o'clock. As I began my ascent to the cemetery I felt a presence by my side. I carried on, feigning an indifference I did not feel. A figure was by my side, dressed I could perceive from the corner of my eye all in black. Then it spoke: 'It is decidedly late for a living soul to be abroad at night.'

I at once recognised the voice to be that of Dr Agar. I turned to him and this impression was confirmed by the evidence of my eyes. He gave a thin smile.

'I have been drawn here by the thread of which you spoke,' I replied.

He nodded thoughtfully. We reached the summit of the steps and entered the graveyard.

'And what is it that you seek, Mr Stoker?' he asked.

I hesitated, unsure of the wisdom of confiding my thoughts. 'To confront my demons,' I said in manner which betrayed my uncertainty of purpose. We stood among the tombstones, looking down towards the harbour.

'Perhaps you wish to conquer whatever you may have previously witnessed here,' he said.

'Perhaps,' I assented.

Dr Agar turned to me. 'If I may presume to offer you the benefit of my experience,' he said in low voice, 'I must tell you that there is nothing here to conquer. There are only stories; stories that we carry in here.' At this point he reached up and prodded me quite forcibly on the temple. 'We can none of us conquer what is inside our own heads. You can no more escape your demons than your demons can escape from you.'

He then gave me a friendly pat on the shoulder and bid me good night. 'It has been a pleasure making your acquaintance, Mr Stoker. When you return to Whitby you must do me the honour of paying me another visit.'

He then turned and made his way back towards the steps. I did not follow him, remaining instead with my back to the church, watching the slow movement of the waves lapping at the harbour walls below. After some minutes, I saw a dark figure emerge on the West Cliff, hurry along to Dr Agar's villa and disappear inside.

Now back in our rooms, an idea is taking shape in my mind. I am not alone here, and as I open a fresh page in my journal, I feel my shadow's hand guiding mine. It only remains for me to give him a name.

Breakynecky

Sarah Moss

IF YOU ARE THINKING OF LEAVING, you should probably go soon.

If you are thinking of leaving, perhaps you should have left, last week or last month or last year. The people who leave first usually fare best.

The depths and surfaces of these waters cradle the bodies of those who left it too late to leave.

Leaving does not make you safe, only safer. You leave when it is safer to go than to stay. By then, nothing is as safe as it was before, when you were little.

It's not that I don't like it here. It's not that I would rather have stayed. I know what happened to those who stayed.

I would rather not have had to leave, that's all. I would rather have been safe where I was, where we all were. Most people, you'll find, would prefer to stay at home, until the dying starts and often for a surprisingly long time, an illogically long time, afterwards.

You should go when you still have people left to leave.

I often walk along the shore, here where the river widens to the sea. I started to say that if you close your eyes it seems like home – like my home, anyway, yours is different – but whatever you can do in your mind it's not that easy to trick the senses into a return. It's not my sea. Between the passing of trains, it can sound like home. The birds, I think, are almost the same as ours, they were born to cross the water the way we might cross a field, and of course the water itself is the same water and it sounds the same, rises and falls the same way on every shore of the world, and the wind, too, in your ears, but it doesn't smell like home where there are turf fires always somewhere on the air and the warm breath of the gorse, and it doesn't feel like home on your skin because the wind here comes from the east, comes over a different sea. We used to see the sunsets, at home, and even with your eyes closed a rising sky is different.

Berwick. Here you are.

It sounded so English. You couldn't imagine them starving in Berwick. I thought of brick houses and coal fires, of roast beef, of pudding. Roofs over people's heads and food on the table; we had nothing to lose. I could be someone's maid, maybe, in a black dress and white apron, or get factory work, set hours and weekly pay. Take it, I said to Séan when they came asking for men, take the work and thank them on your knees. They paid his passage, whoever's at the top, Mr Stephenson or his friends, though of course the money had to come out of Séan's wages. Turned out my mother had a little put by. Enough, more or less. We'll go, I said, we'll cross the water, and Séan paused as if there was a choice.

Anyway, step this way.

We can start here, at the garden. Handy for the station, if you've come that way. Most do. You'll have come for the castle but it's the bridge you'll remember later.

They built the garden a few years ago, in the shadow of the castle. You see the war memorial with the names in alphabetical order, which is the kind of arrangement of grief possible when the disturbance that takes husbands and brothers and sons is far away. There will not be many memorials, at home. Starvation is not heroic. People lose humanity before they die, better not to remember and anyway there were few left to recount the names and none to carve the stones.

Come over, here in the sunshine, a day very much like Séan's.

Step up to the polished stone and trace the names with your fingers. Remember those over the water whose names are written nowhere, those left unburied at the roadsides and on the floors of their houses, those whose faces I could name and those I saw later, on the way to the ship. It is grand to have the name of your beloved written in stone and set up in the garden for remembering the Queen's jubilee. It is grand to be able to do your remembering on public signs, to have people bring red flowers still after a hundred years and not let their dogs piss on your monolith, which is pretty much, as far as I can see, the only outdoor place in England that isn't a convenience for dogs. There's a woman letting her Labrador through the squeaky metal gate; in Séan's time they had the gallows right there. He joined the crowd just once, stood right at the front because it was Patrick they were killing, Patrick who came over with us on the boat, and Séan wanted him to see a friendly face at the last. It was not as if we hadn't seen people die before, plenty of them, both of us, but though they were all going before their time there's a difference between the sins of omission and the sins of commission, between starving half a nation while looking the other way and tying a man's hands, putting a rope around his neck, and dropping the ground beneath his feet.

The dog doesn't like me – they usually don't – and the woman tuts and huffs, reroutes herself to give me a wide berth as if it's the dog who tells her where to go.

Climb the castle mound.

There's a path worn across the grass, mostly by teenagers who come up here in the evenings to smoke and drink, thinking themselves out of sight and brave, too, for haunting the ruins at dusk. As the sun sets and the bottle passes they start trying to frighten each other with stories older than they know: the old man in the tell-tale red cap who lures travellers to his cellar in bad weather. You can't stay out here in this, he says, why don't you come in and wait till it passes, I was about to put the kettle on anyway. And you go in, because why not, because what do you have to lose, because you need shelter and something to eat, and then he'll smash your skull so your blood runs into the ground on which his house is built. They consecrate their homes with strangers' blood in this land, have done time out of mind. Beware the eager host, the goblin red-cap. And the inevitable woman in white, who can be heard and seen sometimes over your shoulder but vanishes when you turn to face her, although why this should be frightening they do not say. Poor woman. People don't make a nuisance of themselves, living or dead, for their own pleasure. Wouldn't we all rather be at rest? It's a fine day and they'll probably be up here later, the young ones, but for now we have the sunny grass and the tenacious tree to ourselves. It should be too steep for trees, and goodness knows what bones and stones its roots grasp below my feet, but here it is, pale blossom under a blue sky. It was not here, back then, has sprung since from some apple core or plum stone chucked into the grass at the end of a picnic. In those days I saw the ground roiled and stabbed, the earth's innards spilling down the hill, turf and trees looking on from the other side of the water and the river itself disturbed, the tides and fish unable to find their old ways up into the land. The young people have left crisp-packets and empty glass bottles; under them, under all, other vessels emptied by other drinkers keeping, or not, watch over the crossing. Roman pots, Rhenish glass, jugs and cups holding the touch of fingers and lips long fallen to dust, gone into the earth from which the blooming tree grows.

Stop, close your eyes, sun yourself.

Sun meant rot, meant blight, meant blackening leaves and hunger. Easter brought hope and summer, fear.

You can climb up to the door-hole and peer in if you want to but there is nothing to see. Shadows and bare ground, bulging stone.

Let's pick our way back down the hill, careful over tussocks, pausing as the wind pushes us back. There are men down at the waterside in bright yellow jackets, remaking the path after winter's storms. The English made our men build roads, even when they could barely stand for hunger and it took hours to move a few rocks: roads going nowhere, roads to take dead feet to abandoned villages, roads to the sea for people whose houses had been pulled down over their heads. These yellow-jacketed men don't need hours, or rocks. The smell of burning oil drifts up the castle mound and the sound of their yolk-yellow machine hammers the afternoon, rattles the teeth in buried skulls. The gate clangs again behind me: another woman, another dog.

The hammering stops and you can hear the water now, and after a shocked silence the rising notes of a curlew, the mew of sandpipers between the rocks and then the keening chorus of gulls. Traffic, somewhere, always. It's always cold along here, always folded into the shade between the hillside and the bridge, the spring always late in reaching these bushes. I pass around the castle's foot, turning as ever to salute the Breakynecky Steps. They rise – or fall – between the sky at the top of the hill and the shore at our feet, see? Hundreds of stone steps dropping like a waterfall, impossibly steep, ruined now but still an invitation of sorts, worn by seven hundred years of human feet hurrying from boats to the castle keep, bringing visitors and weapons and urgent messages, supplies of food and clothes. Nimble, fast. No, no broken necks in my time, not that I saw, and caged off now for the safety of the general public who know no better, who cannot resist sneaking up to fall down, who long, privately, at the backs of their minds, for a little breakynecky. The general public who yearn, just occasionally, for the vertiginous, for gravity, who crave a slip, a flight, a final snap and smash, whose feet know the way to the edge.

I could do it, up and down. Running, even. Sometimes I do. Sometimes someone sees me, a fleet figure, a flicker of shade, up there where you are not allowed to go.

There's another woman with another dog, or perhaps, who knows, the same dog, coming the other way, her eyes too drawn to the breakynecky steps. Not the dog. Dogs have no death wish.

I slip out of the woman's way, through the cold stone tunnel and up the steps to the bench. The men kept watch here almost a millennium, walking up and down to stay awake, boots pacing the limestone slow as a sleeper's heart crossing the night, there and back, there and back, gaze brushing the dark river for an unguarded light or a shape darker than water, for the flutter of a cloak, for outriders and mischief-makers. Vikings, Scots, English: choose your enemy. We used to see the cobles from here, the salmon boats, laid out on the foreshore like fish spread to dry. The castle used to stand implacable against the sky, turreted like the stained glass Jerusalem in the church windows. *And her light was like unto a stone most precious, even like a jasper stone, clear as crystal.* I don't know what colour jasper is. Some kind of sunset, the flames of a clear coal fire. *And the nations of them which are saved shall walk in the light of it: and the kings of the earth do bring their glory and honour into it.* Not all the kings of the earth bring glory and honour. Not all nations are saved. Murderers, you might recall, *shall have their part in the lake which burneth with fire and brimstone.* Some nations, you might think, some kings, are more murderous than others.

And here's the bridge, the miracle of Victorian engineering, like most of Victoria's miracles standing on the blood and bones of those who built it. You passed over it on the train, but of course you can't see a bridge while you cross it. Here's the duck's eye, fish's eye view. It rises over us like a cathedral, as if a boy could stand under it and sing, as if prayer might drift like incense under the arches, and indeed the smell of tar comes on the wind from the workmen downriver. Always there's been work along here, all the years hammering and pounding, breaking rock and gouging earth, hacking trees, rabbits' burrows sliced open like houses in a war and worms exposed like spilled guts. In the end they had to use dynamite on the castle, had to invade their own town. It could almost be a joke. You could feel the charge in the earth and in your bones, the air rang and buildings jerked right over the other side of the town, though it was only the latest bombardment of many. The English have to assault themselves when no-one else will do it.

Come back down to the path. You hear trains before you see them, down here, or maybe, since the water is loud against the pilings and the gulls are loud in the air and the curlews loud on the rocks, you feel the trains. They're not much, compared to the bridge. The bridge needs the old trains, the dragon trains breathing fire and winging their way across the land. Stephenson imagined this bridge for shrieking and roaring, for the opera of steam and iron pistons and a whistling cry of the sort a person might hear by night as a presentiment of death, not the coy slither of red and grey in which the engine looks the same as the carriages. Few of the trains stop here now, now the coal has gone and the salmon and the herring, now they don't make pantiles or grow grain or spin wool, now there's nothing to send.

We restless ones mass, sometimes, there at the hinge point, the portal where the sea touches the river and the bridge strikes the land, where they built the castle over the fort over the oldest dwelling place, and where they broke the castle for the trains. It's dangerous, I said, when Séan showed me why we were here, and he thought I meant there'd be men hurt and killed in the work, but that danger was too obvious to say, we all knew that, that was why they had us come over for it. I meant that it's dangerous to go digging and smashing a place where people have been in fear, where they've been shut up and hurt, where bodies have been broken in the name of money and land, these seven centuries. Of course when you bring down the walls they might land on your head but you know the masters have thought of that, included the loss of a few men in their plans. They hadn't thought of those they were disturbing, the ancient ones who were still there when the navvies came with their dynamite and picks. Ah, that old stuff, Séan said, and sure these are men of science, Mary, none of that, do you know the trains will be running all the way to London, Edinburgh to London in one day? I'd have to have been deaf not to know that, the times he said it. Sure, I said, even so, you'll want to watch what you're about.

And it was the stones that took him, of course, a few weeks later. They, his mates, were a long time finding me, hours in which he was dying and then dead and I didn't know, hours in which others, his workmates and the bosses, knew what had happened to him and to me, and I, elbow-deep in steaming smalls at the laundry, thinking that perhaps if I caught her in a bright moment Mrs Hadfield would let me nip out to the market before it closed for some bacon for Séan's tea, did not know. They were waiting for me when I came home, Mick and Iain, standing at the door as if already before the coffin with their heads bowed and their caps in their hands, silent. I knew, really, as soon as I saw them there, felt my heart drop to the cobbles under my feet as the bright day wavered around my eyes and ears. A cat crossed the street, a fat tortoise-shell I hadn't seen before. They stepped forward. Mrs O'Driscoll, Mick said, Mary, we've bad news for you, and I found myself sitting not even on my doorstep but on the street, legs folded under me because it was too late, now, to run to him, to sponge his face and say the words to carry him over, because there was nothing I could do for him. I heard a great cry rise in the late afternoon warmth, between the walls and the sunny roofs. Ah, they said, come now, Mary, come into the house. He didn't suffer, Mick kept saying while Iain lit the stove and set the water to boil, you must know that, Mary, it came so quick, he never spoke or moved after. Yes, I said, yes, thank you, and in my head I saw the rocks, the great walls set also in the blood of working men seven hundred years ago, shocked and tumbling. Stones should not fly. Rock is not meant for the air.

Dust we are and to dust we shall return.

And the walls came tumbling down.

Later, towards sunset, after I'd persuaded Mick and Iain and the kind and curious neighbours to leave me, I came down here. I came past where they were already building the station on the site of the Great Hall, setting the platforms in place of the gallery and laying the rails over the flagged floor and the fireplace in which oxen had been roasted. Waiting and fire, still, metal and flames and the slow passing of time. The Jubilee Garden was then a ravine with a millstream through it, and I climbed down the side of the water and then over the rocks on the shoreline, between the falling castle and the rising bridge. I had seen Séan's body by then. They wouldn't uncover his face. I knew what I was looking for and after a while, the sky dimming and the birds settling for the brief night, I found it.

The sun had been so bright that the marks had already dried iron-red, the colour of the peats in summer. I began to gather the stones but I couldn't lift all of them and there had been very much blood, pooled and still dark where it had run down into the damp shade, sticky on my fingers. I knew that, that a body can spray and trickle and pour more blood than seems possible for its size, but still I tried at least to map the boundaries, to see where my husband's blood had not been spilt, to find the margin of unspotted ground. There was hair, too, on the big rock, and I crouched and then knelt, grasped it in my arms, felt it crush my breasts and graze my breastbone and ribs as I strained to raise it.

They are too heavy. There are too many stones here, flecked and splashed and stained with too much blood. I can't hold them all, even in my mind.

It's the walls that kill you, not the ghosts. Séan was right, the dead have no power to harm, and none to heal either.

The Loathly Lady

Fiona Mozley

1

LYTHE AND LISTENYTHE THE LIF OF A LORD RICHE (was there ever another kind?). While he was alive, there was no one else like him in the world. Royal and courteous, of all the kings, Arthur was the flower, and his knights were chivalrous and brave.

King Arthur hunts in Inglewood with the knights of his court. It is a no-place: too far north for the English (though they have given it their name); too far south for the Scots (though they have been here once or twice). Huntsmen spot a hart in a thicket of bracken. Hounds bray, horses gallop. The deer hears the clamour and stands dead still.

Clothed in green in a blinking wood, leaves like eyelids, fluttering, flickering. Green like sunshine, green like night. A wood, a hart, the once and future king. They have been here before, they will come here again. He will follow a beast and it will follow him. They will evince, they will evade, they will venture, they will vanquish, they will dance, they will court, they will wrestle, they will sing.

Arthur, alone, sees the hart's mind, and tells his companions he will stalk the deer, and catch it by stealth and not by chase. He creeps beneath branches, between trunks. He tip-toes on tree roots, and scuffs the woodland loam.

Arthur is everything and nothing, has everything, has no one, wants (for) nothing, desires a world. He is boy-king, man-boy, woods-man. He is king of these woods; he is a king who would.

And wodmanly he stowpyd lowe. He stalks the deer for half a mile. His retinue is now far off. Through green sunshine, he spots an eye, spots it once then once again, then a haunch, and a flash of a white tail. His bow is made from yew, taken from a tree older than this story. The arrow is willow with fletchings from a goose. The bowstring is gut; it snaps a reaction. The arrow takes flight. The iron points blood.

An animal falls once and once again, and vanishes into a cloud of green fern. Arthur leaps to the spot, marked now by rising spores, and kneels by the deer, as if in reverence to a dying monarch. He will dress the animal with his own kingly hands, take its skin, cut its flesh. He will serve it well, and taste the fat.

But as Arthur stalked the deer, he was stalked himself. There was another in Inglewood. The other stepped; the other crept. He came upon Arthur. An unknown knight places a blade at the nape of the kneeling king.

If the man is a knight; the knight is a brute. Larger than is rightly right, with arms and legs like lumber, and a belly like a pregnant sow. His helmet bears antlers, and his armour – plate and mail – is twisted and knotted around his frame as if they are grafted and grown together. His face is covered by a visor. He lifts it and Arthur sees skin sunken with sores, a swollen nose, and blooded eyes.

'King Arthur.' The knight greets the king discourteously. 'You have done me wrong more than once and once again. I have waited for you in these woods, and now I find you alone, without your knights, without your court.'

'Who are you and what do you want?'

'I am Sir Somer Gromer Joure. You took my lands and gave them to your nephew, Sir Gawain. Now I have no lands, and I walk in the wilderness like a wilder-man.'

King Arthur has no memory of this knight, though Sir Gromer has a face and a shape that might be termed memorable. Still, Arthur has no weapon except his bow, and he wears no armour, only green cloth. His only defence in this wood is against sight, and he has been seen.

'I am in your power. What can I give you so that you will let me live? I have a kingdom that depends on me. I have a future.'

'There's not much you can offer me. Now I am accustomed to my life in the woods I want neither land nor gold. But there is a certain thing, which you can do for me. If, of course, you agree.'

'What is it?' asks the king, impatient to be on his feet.

'You must agree before I tell you what it is.'

'But how can I do that? It might be an impossible thing.'

'Then I will have to kill you,' says Sir Gromer, gleefully, taking hold of the hilt of his sword with both his broad hands.

'No, wait,' pleads the king. 'I agree, I agree.'

'On your honour?' asks the knight.

'On my honour as a king,' Arthur replies.

'Then I shall accept your word, and let you live.' Sir Somer Gromer sheaths his blade and stretches out his arm towards the kneeling king. Arthur takes the knight's hand and rises to his feet. He stands only to his chest. The king is small against this man.

Then Sir Gromer says: 'Now that you are standing, I will tell you what it is you have sworn to. In twelve months, to the day, you must meet me by the cross that stands in this wood. You must come alone, without any of your lords or your knights. You must tell no one you are coming, and you must tell no one about this meeting. You must bring with you one thing, and one thing only – the answer to a question: what do women want? If you bring me no answer, you will lose your head.'

Arthur is woo.

It is an impossible task; an absurd question without an answer. It is a nothing, a nowhere, a never. But he swore on his honour, his honour as a king. And Arthur's honour is worth his life, and Arthur's life is worth a once and future kingdom.

The knight smiles. He reveals blackened teeth sharpened to a point, like a lion or a wolf or a bear. Something bestial, something not-man. 'Go, then,' he says. 'Your life is in my hands.'

Arthur puts his bugle to his lips and blows, though his breath is less than it should have been. The unknown knight disappears into the thick of the wood, folding himself between trees like a sea-shell between waves. He's there, then he's gone, he's there, he's there, then he's gone, then he's there, then he's gone, he's gone, he's gone.

2

Arthur's retinue arrives to see only the king and the deer, and Arthur says nothing of his meeting. The court returns to Carlisle, to a stone castle standing perpendicular, straight and predictable against the ellipses and fractals of moors and trees. The stones are the colours of a Carlisle sky, fog and mist and cloud made solid and still. There are towers for seeing, and towers for being seen. There are dark corners for hiding and forgetting, and wide halls for the eating ritual, the public performance of devouring. There are walls to keep out the Scots. There are walls to keep out the English. There are walls to keep out the wild.

That evening, Arthur holds the events of the day in his heart's mind. He cannot enjoy the feast. The deer has become roast venison. Turned on a spit above a fire, the animal's nature is forever changed, like a base metal in the hands of an alchemist. The cooks bring Arthur the richest cut, but it sits on his plate untouched, while his lords consume their own portions, and squires and pages gnaw on bones.

One of the knights is the king's nephew. Sir Gawain is a sensitive young man, handsome and brave, the most courteous of all the king's knights. While everyone else is busy eating, he notices the demeanour of his uncle. He sees that he is not devouring the deer as he should, and he is alarmed. If a king does not eat his meat, he is not king at all.

After the feast, Gawain goes to Arthur's chamber. It is the highest room in the castle, placed there so Arthur can do the most seeing and be the most seen. Gawain climbs the many stairs, placing his feet on the grooves that have been made by feet before his own, or perhaps of future feet, stepping once and once again. He finds his uncle there alone (Arthur does have a wife, but who knows where she's got to).

Arthur tells Gawain about the meeting in the forest. He tells him of the deer, the knight, and the bargain. 'No answer can possibly be found,' Arthur moans. 'In twelve months I must return to the place of our meeting, and I will lose either my head or my honour.'

Gawain has experience of bargains struck, of twelve-month promises, and the honest proffering of a neck for a woodsman's axe. And Gawain is of the view that any unanswered question requires a quest.

'You have been asked a question, so now you must go on a quest. The further we travel, the more we will learn. We will seek knowledge with swords out-stretched. If I come too, we will double our chances of finding an answer. You go in one direction and ask everyone you meet. I will go in another direction and ask everyone I meet. We will write our answers on paper, and when we return we shall compile the pages into a book.'

Arthur agrees. Though he has little hope, there is nothing

else he can think to do. The next morning, the two men set off on their journeys. Each follows his own road. They ask every person they meet what it is that women want.

'What do they want what do they want what do they want?'

King Arthur and Sir Gawain receive many answers: enough to fill two books. Some tell them that women want gold. Some tell them women want never to grow old. Some say women want a burly man to hold. The king and the knight quest for eleven months, but when they return and compare what they have learned, neither man is satisfied they have the answer to save the king.

'I have only one month until I must return to the forest and offer myself up to be butchered. Nothing in these books will do. It's all lost – my kingdom, my life. All because I was tracked through the forest. I was so intent on catching that hart, I was caught myself. Unarmed and unaware. I should have taken the blow, and never agreed to this challenge.'

Arthur is fulle woo. Gawain remains hopeful. 'You still have a month. Ride out again, this time into the forest, and see what you find.'

With nothing to lose and nowhere else to go, Arthur returns to Inglewood. He follows the paths as he followed before, he followed the paths he will follow again. Past trees as tall as ships, green darkness and green light.

He comes to the place the deer was slain and sees what looks at first like a woodsman on a horse, but as he gets closer, and closer again, he sees that it isn't a woodsman but a woman. And as he gets closer and closer again, he sees the foulest, ugliest, most woody woman he has ever seen. She is the most repulsive creature in the knotted wood, the most repulsive creature in the known world. Her face is all red and raw. Her nose is snotty. Her mouth is wide and her teeth are yellow, hanging out of her mouth over her lips. Her cheeks are as wide as a woman's hips, and her hips and breasts are as large as those of a horse.

Her horse, Arthur observes, is, however, quite charming. It is a pretty beast draped in fine cloth, adorned with gold and precious stones. How strange, he reflects, for such an ugly woman to be riding such a dainty horse. He sees the woman and is repulsed. He sees the horse and is captivated.

Arthur steadies his own stallion at the sight of this glorious mare (or is his a mare and hers a stallion?) and he asks the woman, 'What do you want?'

'My name is Dame Ragnelle, and I have come here to help, or at least to strike a bargain so that we might both be helped. I can give you the answer to the question you have been asked. If you agree to my demands I will tell you the answer. If you do not agree, you will leave this forest no wiser and you will return to it in one month and lose your head.'

King Arthur, for the most part, kept his promise to Sir Gromer, and told no one of their meeting, except Gawain. He is therefore startled that this unknown woman knows of their deal.

'What do you want in return?'

'I wish to wed a knight at your court. I have heard about him. They say he is the most courteous knight that has ever lived, and I have fallen in love with him from afar.'

There is only one knight she can mean. Arthur knows who it is before she tells him. He cringes at the thought of his beautiful and handsome nephew marrying this monster, though he knows that Gawain would not hesitate if it were to save the life of his king.

'Is there no other way? Could you not just give me the answer and leave my nephew alone?'

'There is no other way. If you promise to this demand, I shall tell you what it is that women want. And if that answer proves to be the one that saves your life, I shall come to your court and wed Sir Gawain in front of all your lords and ladies. Do you agree?'

Reluctantly, Arthur agrees: his life is not his alone, but belongs to a kingdom. Dame Ragnelle leans forward, like lovers lean to kiss. Her breath is rancid. It sweeps over his face and neck like vinegar poured to pickle him whole. He shuts his eyes and she whispers in his ear.

King Arthur stands back, amazed. He must not have heard correctly. He asks her to repeat herself, and she whispers the answer for a second time. Again, he is sure he has misheard. Either there has been mishearing or misunderstanding.

It takes a third telling for Arthur to believe that he caught her words as she meant to speak them. He lets out a single, low laugh. Then he laughs again, and soon he cannot stop laughing, and the trees around him begin to shake in the wind as if they are laughing too. Ragnelle's answer is absurd. It is ridiculous. There is no way that it is the answer he needs. Gawain is safe from this woman and her abominable proposal.

King Arthur rides back to Carlisle Castle. At first, he is relieved. It would have been a horrible sight, to see his lovely nephew marry such a monster. Then he starts to worry. He is sure Ragnelle's answer is not the right answer, but then which one is it?

When he gets back, he tells Gawain about his meeting, and everything she said to him. Gawain does not laugh with his uncle, but simply nods, and tells him he will do his duty.

3

On the prescribed day, twelve months from the day of the fateful hunt, Arthur rides out to Inglewood Forest for the third time. He rides through a palisade of trees with thick branches packed in defence. He rides past herds of deer – does, harts, stags – that at other times, he has hunted, and which he hopes to hunt again.

Arthur rides alone, with no armour and no sword, clothed only in green, his cloak no thicker than the hide of a hind. He meets Sir Gromer at the carved wooden cross, which stands at a crossroads in a clearing. Sir Gromer's sword is drawn before him, held in both hands, tip rooted in the green earth. Arthur approaches him as if knight is king and king is knight. He is ready to bend his neck to the blade.

Sir Gromer: 'Come, Sir King. Tell me, what do women want?'

Arthur pulls out the two volumes he and Gawain compiled. He passes them both to the monstrous knight. Sir Gromer devours the books as a hawk devours its prey, reading each page then ripping it from its binding and tossing it over his shoulder to be caught by the wind and returned to the wood. As he reads, he mutters: 'No, no, no.' As he finishes the last of the pages, he bellows: 'No, no, no!' He tosses the empty books away, and raises his sword. 'Sir King, you are a dead man. I will cut off your head and hack you limb from limb and joint you and skin you and hang you in my larder and make mince from your heart and lungs and make strings for my bow from your guts.'

'Wait,' says King Arthur, realising he must use the answer given to him by Dame Ragnelle, and thus bind his friend to that awful woman forever. 'I have one last possible answer that I did not write down.'

'Tell it to me then. Why delay?'

'I will tell you, then,' he says, readying himself. 'The thing that women want,' he says. 'The thing that women want,' he says once again. 'The thing that they desire. The thing that they would choose, choose above all the things written in those books, above wealth and health and love. That thing they would choose, it is choice itself.'

Sir Gromer pulls up his sword again as if to strike the king, but instead he thrusts it into the wooden cross, where it gets stuck. He shouts and curses King Arthur, and kicks his boots against the dirt. 'That woman who told you,' he rages. 'I would like to see that woman burn on a fire. And that woman, Dame

Ragnelle, is my sister.'

Sir Gromer continues to rail against his sister, but there is nothing he can do. He wanted to trap King Arthur and kill him, but now he must let him go. The woodland knight returns to his woodland keep and King Arthur begins to ride back to the castle at Carlisle, with its high stone walls and perpetual feasting, but as he had feared, he has not gone far before he meets Dame Ragnelle, the hideous woman on her beautiful horse.

'You used my answer and it saved your life,' she says to him. 'Now you must allow me to ride with you back to Carlisle, where I shall marry Sir Gawain. He is my choice.'

And so, the famous king rides with this winsome woman, wishing she were further from him and not at his side. At Carlisle, Gawain meets his bride, and true to his nature, he greets her with respect. From his face alone, nobody can know what he sees. They marry right away (better it were done quickly) and afterwards there is a feast.

Ragnelle eats all she is given, and she is given more. She eats all the more, and is given more and more again. She pulls at the bleeding meat with her hands, her long nails tearing like talons, her yellow teeth gnashing like fangs.

The beautiful and courteous lords and ladies of the court stare. *So fowlle a sowe sawe nevere man.* Many of them weep at the thought of their beloved Gawain married to this hag. But Gawain sits next to his bride and talks and laughs with her between mouthfuls of meat, and nobody could know from his actions what it is that he sees.

After the feasting, Dame Ragnelle and Sir Gawain go together to his bed chamber. Now, all the lords and ladies of the court weep (or do they laugh?) at the thought of Gawain in bed with this ugly witch. They throw back their heads in hysteria. Gawain and Ragnelle are born aloft by the bellowing and screaming. It carries them up the winding stairs.

The wife lies on the bed and turns away from her husband.

'I know that I am hideous,' she says. 'I am happy to have married you, and you have done everything you should have at dinner. But I cannot ask you to do everything that a husband does with a wife. I am content for us just to live together. We do not have to have sex, if you don't want to. It's your choice.'

'I chose to be your husband,' Gawain replies. 'I choose to do everything with you that a husband does with a wife. If it is your choice too.'

Dame Ragnelle turns back towards her husband and she is suddenly beautiful. Her features have retreated, her teeth have shrunk and turned bright white, her hands are no longer claws. She is suddenly as beautiful as she was ugly before. Gawain is amazed. His amazement can be read plainly on his face. *He sawe her the fayrest creature that evere he sawe.*

'Jesus Christ, what are you?'

'I am your wife.'

'Yes, but you are beautiful. Just a minute ago, you were the ugliest woman I have ever seen. Forgive me if I'm unable to remain entirely calm.' Gawain sits down on the bed with his wife. He is unable to stand it; he is unable to stand.

'You have another choice to make,' she tells him. 'Either I am ugly during the day, when all the world can see me, and beautiful at night, when only you can see me, or I am beautiful in the day when all the world can see me, and ugly at night when only you can see me. You must either go to bed with an ugly woman or have the world believe that you are going to bed with an ugly woman. You must either go to bed with a beautiful woman or have the world believe you are going to bed with a beautiful woman. Which is it, Gawain?'

Gawain says nothing for a while. Perhaps he is considering his options. If he is, he gives no signs. He is immobile, implacable, resolute. Then he takes her hand, and says: 'The choice is yours to make.'

Dame Ragnelle smiles, and rises to kiss him. 'That is the right answer,' she says. 'I was cursed,' she explains. 'I was cursed by my step-mother. She was an evil bitch. She transfigured me into the woman you saw before and told me that nothing would lift the spell except the love of a courteous man. And now that you have not only married me but treated me with respect, though you thought I was the most hideous thing you had ever seen, the curse will be lifted, and I will be beautiful all the time.'

'Great,' he says, and they get into bed.

Here endythe the weddyng of
Syr Gawen and Dame Ragnelle
For helpyng of Kyng Arthoure.

Capture

Adam Thorpe

'TELL ME ABOUT THE CASTLE,' said Louisa, wishing it had more shadow to it.

Her cousin William turned and cried, 'You don't want to know, Lou!' He was adopting a dramatic pose, arms flung out, the sea just beyond him. Louisa immediately realised that he knew absolutely nothing about the place. Hugh, his friend from Charterhouse, making up the expedition's foursome along with Dorothy, would even pronounce it wrongly, with a hard 'g'. Tintaggle!

'Why won't I want to know?' She set her brush chiming prettily in the water-bowl, clouds of cerulean blue billowing out like the myth of a Cornish summer. William wasn't hand-some, precisely, but then he wasn't plain, either. She knew this from the judgements of her friends over the years and es-pecially those of Dorothy. Dorothy had suggested the trip to Cornwall in the first place. It was Dorothy, in fact, who had resolved the absence of chaperones by recruiting her own uncle and aunt – Aunt Becka and Uncle Jack. William had faint hairs, a kind of juvenile suggestion of maleness, delicately sketched on the end of his chin, but his jacket smelt of rich tobacco.

'Because it is ugly,' he said. 'Knights hacking away at each other with swords like cleavers.'

Louisa laughed, deliberately surprising him. 'What a lark,' she cried.

She saw, in one of her customary vivid flashes, huge men covered in dark plates clanking and shouting, the occasional limb sliced through, blood jetting out onto the grass which sprouted on the broken walls as well as underfoot. Then the smaller sounds came into her ears: a grunting, a cursing, the splash of life blood on the stones and the flower-strewn earth. Mostly it terrified and disgusted her, although a morsel of it thrilled. She recognised none of the words that came to her: it wasn't English, nor was it French. Maybe it was Cornish, which was no longer a living language save in the mouths of very old and mostly unfriendly folk.

Louisa wanted to leave this spot as you leave a shadowy corner near damp rocks. She had the curious sensation that the corner was pursuing her on thin legs, even though she was going nowhere. She was very much installed on the ruined wall, with her cushion, her portable materials in their little wooden suitcase, small rolls of canvas and her sketchbook. The wind was blustery, as it probably always was here on the westernmost promontory of the British Isles. Yet she felt the dampness. She felt it sliding down her throat like a horrible medicine.

'William,' she enquired, 'how long do you wish to stay?'

'Well,' he glanced at his pocket-watch, 'a little more than twenty minutes!'

'Twenty minutes?'

'The extent of our sojourn here this morning so far.'

That was impossible. She had already stayed a lifetime. Two hours at least. The breeze had brushed her bones. She had completed several feeble sketches and William had smoked his pipe down to the ash.

She was bored by his teasing. Suddenly she asked, as if

wanting to show she was unimpressed by it, 'How old is the castle?'

William shifted on his little folding chair. He had no idea, evidently. To most people, the ruins were like any other ruins: heaps of stone blocks loosely cemented together by a sort of ancient, crumbling mortar into precarious walls, chunks bitten out of them like traces of hungry rats in cheese, the grass – along with clumps of wild garlic or bluebells or red campion – shivering and shaking beneath ancient mullions and sprouting from loaves of sand-worn sills. Where there was a roof, the slate tiles looked ready to slide off onto innocent heads. Seagulls occupied any available space like flapping sheets of used blotting paper, then wheeled away in the stronger gusts that occasionally had the two of them seizing their work, the wetter patches of watercolour sending dark worms of colour across the paper, to remain for good once dry.

William, by all but refusing to paint, idling with his pipe, made her feel over-zealous. Yet Louisa knew that he was a jolly good painter, able to describe anything (from rocks to a stormy sea) in a mere handful of strokes, whether the brush was laden or scratchy. It was unfair, as if lassitude and laziness were in league with the appropriate gods.

'William, I am growing cold. This is not a place for sitting still.'

'Not even for a few minutes?'

She had initially ignored his teasing, but now the irritation began to swirl in too fiercely. He had a persistent, rather dull way of teasing which grew vexatious, like an inflammation. 'I wish it *had* been a mere few minutes. Instead, we have fixed ourselves here to no great effect for well over an hour.'

He laughed again, reaching into his jacket's top pocket and glancing at the handsome fob on its thin chain. 'According to my grandfather's timepiece,' he persisted, 'it is twenty minutes since we unfolded our stools and set to.' The watchchain glinted in the abrupt sunshine. Gleefully, it seemed to Louisa.

She bent her head a little, tucking stray elements of her pinned-up hair back into place. His persistence was embarrassing. She had her own elegant watch on her wrist, as flat as a tapeworm, but she had forgotten to check it on arrival. The watch was new, a gift from her dear godmother, and she was not yet accustomed to it. She had, however, glanced at her wrist at some point after starting to paint, when (this being the phrase that trotted gaily and repeatedly through her mind, like a refrain in a musical comedy) she was already bored and not a little chilled. Three o'clock, it had said. Now it was announcing past four o'clock and her shawl was no match for the colder gusts, and her legs under the long thick skirt had cramp. 'And is twenty minutes,' she ventured, 'your threshold of tolerance?'

'Tolerance of what?'

'Of sitting on a blowy clifftop with your imminent fiancée?' Her eyes slid towards him and, if she wasn't mistaken, she saw the beginnings of a blush.

It was clear that her favourite cousin recognised that she wasn't being serious, that it was the usual 'giddy' Louisa at play to snag his attention, but that to have laughed would have been rude. She was dropped on her head by accident when only a few months old by her *ayah* in Calcutta and rumours of a bruise on the brain persisted. It was all nonsense, of course – that she was in any way damaged! – but she knew the family maintained their doubts. Her occasional eccentricities passed without remark, which gave her a certain advantage. He was confused because he was so fond of her (and perhaps in love with her) that her quirks evidently seemed to him an integral part of his affection.

A sudden glow of bright sun passed over his face, of which she felt the warmth soon enough, and was then obliterated by a cloud. She was enjoying her customary spell of power, brief and curious: being able to control her cousin's feelings, to touch them, prod them out of the shadows would always thrill her with this deep pleasure, rare though it was. She had not felt this as a child, meeting William for the first time, the little blonde boy only a year or two younger than herself, when she was freshly returned from India. They had met several times a year since, which made them an occasional fixture to each other, like a jovial tennis match, between long anecdotal letters. A fixture, nevertheless, to anticipate with a gentle pulse of pleasure.

Today, when the four of them had formed into pairs well over an hour ago, agreement had been reached. She and William were to capture in their sketchbooks the castle and its grassy grounds (really, just tumbled stones losing the race over centuries to wild Nature and the sea-churning elements), Dorothy and Hugh to compose Tennysonian poems. Their chaperones were reading compact, grave-looking books in which feathers had been inserted to mark pages, occasionally glancing in their direction for duty's sake, because they were in a world of cliffs and heaving sea. But these two elders in their heavy and voluminous dark togs were not only well out of earshot, as everything was – thanks to the sea crashing below – they were also mostly out of sight around the rocky corner. Almost a symbolic presence, in fact.

At moments, Louisa imagined the entire promontory as being swept free of people, followed by the rest of the island of Britain, and then terra firma in general.

That evening, like the one before, they took it in turns to read aloud in front of a roaring wood fire in the stolid, brand new King Arthur Hotel with its soft carpets and brightly coloured murals, while Dorothy's aunt and uncle were again nodding in a similitude of appreciation. Louisa had no interest whatsoever in William as her future personified, nor in his dull poems, but simply as an endearing and much-loved relation. Yet there was a faint suggestion in the whole thing of audacity, of possibility.

'Look at the coloured light splashing on the wall,' she

abruptly pointed out: the fire was bright enough to dance on the bare stone walls of this large communal room where the modern tapestries had left the viewer an area of imaginative grace. The smell of burning logs and thick wool carpets mingled confusingly with Dorothy's over-applied jasmine scent. All their cheeks glowed.

Hugh stirred in his faux-medieval chair with its high back, his neck garlanded with red spots from the skin rubbing on his starched collar, cradling a delicate balloon of ginger ale and brandy. 'Where do you think this fellow, Earl Richard, slept?' He had turned towards Dorothy, who frowned back. Louisa wished his pronunciation of his 'rs' had more sinew. As it was, each threatened to crumble like a ripple in dry sand.

'Nowhere in this room,' Louisa quickly replied for Dorothy, whose knowledge of the place and Arthurian history in general was self-confessedly thin, 'as the place did not exist in the twelfth century.'

William chuckled. 'Built last year,' he nodded. His ambition, Louisa knew, was to be an architect and build homes fit for (very wealthy) lords.

Hugh looked up sharply. 'Of course I knew that. It's the spit of our new block in Charterhouse, as it happens. But if the room *had* existed back then ...'

Hugh had turned his stupidity into a jesting game. That's how these boys escaped consequences. The wind off the sea was like a gently scolding mother, slapping the building but never with real violence. It made the pale, freshly carved mullioned windows shudder, and puffed bitter smoke from the fireplace into the room by way of the ornate chimney. Aunt Becka had nodded off and was now lightly snoring. Until someone smiled at this, it would be embarrassing. Nobody volunteered.

The following day, they departed the hotel on a breakfast of eggs and kippers and returned to Tintagel Castle using the new, cemented footpath, each armed with a sturdy local walk-

ing stick. Their guardians were absent, as Aunt Becka had declared herself ill from an oyster and Uncle Jack wished to stay
and care for her. A hotel servant, bearded like a pirate with
saltworn cheeks and a somewhat gruff temperament, accompanied them instead. The steps, albeit of clean white concrete,
still felt perilous to anyone with a poor head for heights: the
sea swayed and crashed into foam far below, the silhouetted
ruin might have been made of sand on a beach. They passed
what appeared to be an original wall of dark stone (a fragment
that included an ancient timeworn window), then a complete
hut with its slates mostly intact, crouching at the base of the
castle's remains like the home of a primitive Briton in the days
of the Round Table.

'The ancient groundsman's cottage,' Hugh suggested,
without a trace of irony, which made the others laugh.

'What's so amusing?' he asked, in a miffed tone.

'I fear that the girls think you are too thoroughly trapped in
modern times,' William suggested, sparking a further round of
laughter from everyone but Hugh (and the Cornishman, who
was sucking with intensity on his clay pipe). A reminder of
the kippers suddenly broke into Louisa's mouth like an unwelcome guest. She felt faintly out of breath, as if she had a lung
condition. Which she most decidedly did not have.

Their party, as determined as any Alpine expedition, was
now tackling the steeper steps, mounting the rock in zig-zag
fashion accompanied by squeaks of the metal frame bolted
to the cliff. It was a little daring, physically: the servant was
clearly stretching them, or else he was ignorant of the true
capacities of gentlefolk, or he wished their numbers reduced.
The party stopped and stood in a line holding tight to the
hand-rail that saved any foolhardy visitors from slipping over,
while Louisa – being the appointed literary expert – shouted
out the story of Tristan and Iseult above the wind. Their questions were posed as if they were all on a school outing, which
caused great mirth. The first was the difference between the

names Isolde and Iseult. There was none at all, or not one that meant anything beyond matters of spelling. Hugh's questioning sounded sluggish.

'Who was this ... Iseult?' The name came out shakily.

'The wife of Morholt of Ireland,' Louisa said. She wished they could move on from a spot that felt steep and perilous.

Dorothy asked: 'How did she become the betrothed of Tristan?'

'After Morholt's defeat,' Louisa's voice was now barely audible even to herself over the smashing of the waves, 'she was sent for by Tristan's uncle, King Mark of Cornwall, who intended to marry her. She had, of course, no say in the matter: these were primitive times, many hundreds of years ago.' She suddenly felt cross, as if she were reliving a story she had personally experienced. Why should men be always so authoritative?

'So King Mark gave Tristan the task of fetching Iseult from Ireland,' she continued. 'One has to imagine boats fluttering flags, a proper royal escort, all that sort of jolly caper.'

'Which would be very satisfying,' William said, shielding his eyes from a dazzle that suddenly crossed his face like a theatre light, 'if the escorted happened to be oneself.'

Dorothy looked genuinely chilled, with a blue-tinted nose. She was gripping the rail with gloved fingers. Hugh's eyes were closed in apparent private meditation.

'King Mark's young nephew,' Louisa went on, enjoying herself at last, as if her audience had grown large and captivated, 'was barely older than Iseult herself.' She was shouting above the surf, which was trying to scale the cliffs with foamy white fingers. 'On the way, a mischievous elf called Dill' – she had invented this agreeable detail, as was her wont – 'slipped a love potion into the two young people's drink.'

Dorothy blushed and William had grown visibly uncomfortable. Hugh did not react at all. Could this be, Louisa mused – not without a pulse of jealousy – the stage curtain twitching open on a secret? (She had fallen for Hugh last year in London, having watched him play a terrific game of Old Carthusians' rugby at Charterhouse, and then promptly recovered from the madness on sitting opposite him at dinner, where his capacity for making remarks as hearty as they were empty was on display.) She had now adopted the theatrical stance of someone reciting lines of poetry, an art which she had learnt at her own intimate little school in Hampstead, and began a recitation which was repeatedly snatched away by the sea-crash.

None, unless the saints above,
Knew the secret of their love ...

William started clapping prematurely, as if Louisa's delivery had suggested a climax, but she glowered at him with such intensity that he immediately desisted, blinking in embarrassment. The gulls screeching over the swaying brine were showing an equal lack of respect for literary performance.

'When King Mark discovered his wife's adultery, he was frightfully cross, understandably. He wished to execute the couple by hanging and burning.' Louisa had forgotten who was to suffer which punishment. She hoped no one would notice. Dorothy spoke up, but only to remark on the cruelty of those times and to say she very much hoped it was time for tea and scones.

'Naturally,' Louisa continued, ignoring this, and feeling the ribbons frantically rippling at her neck, 'Tristan escaped on the way to execution, and snatched Iseult from the jaws of danger.'

'Hooray,' cried Dorothy, and swept her arm dramatically over the sea's horizon, the effect reduced by the sudden change of bright summer weather into a cool greyness announcing rain, as if all Cornwall's phantoms had clustered to observe them.

Not waiting for any questions – it was obvious that her audience was lost in the expectation of tea – Louisa explained that Tristan, finally, if reluctantly, had agreed with King Mark to yield Iseult and leave the country.

She had first read the legend in a large, illustrated book in her father's voluminous library, but she had soon lost her childish attraction to the knight who gave up his loved one.

A surviving carved fragment of the castle's doorjamb suddenly and theatrically, as if not quite by chance, lay under her hand, a tear in the clouds sweeping it into view. It seemed astonishing, it seemed to drag her deeper into the impossibly distant past. The pinkish surface of the pockmarked relic reminded her of something: their chaperone Uncle Jack's fleshy face. Slow-witted Hugh (Louisa had never *diagnosed* him thus, as it were, until a few seconds ago) abruptly sat down on the cement steps and clamped his eyes shut, shivering. The wind had dropped, leaving their ears clearer.

William seemed to agree with her. He declared that he considered the knight to have been disgustingly weak; Hugh – eyes still shut tight – was cautiously supportive, but Dorothy objected: had Tristan refused to yield to King Mark's demands the young lovers would have been executed, which would have been too dreadful. 'Now may we have our tea and scones?'

The recently constructed path to the refreshments cabin rounded a corner of the cliff-face where almost immediately they entered a relative quietude, as if stepping into a church. To either side were shivering, secretive patches of bluebells in dips in the terrain. It occurred to Louisa how dull their lives were, so dull she felt embarrassed to be in the presence of these rocks and clifftops and crashing waters, which had serious duties to fulfil. Beside her Dorothy remarked how much more heroic and noble those times were. Louisa nodded. 'Such brave fellows in those days,' Dorothy sighed, glancing at William and Hugh. Hugh was apparently set on planting his feet with slow, intense accuracy and made no comment.

'Your hand is unusually fine-boned, Lou,' Dorothy pointed out.

Maybe I am growing quietly ill, Louisa thought. She herself had never mused upon the shape or size of any of her friends' hands before – for a start, she had never tried drawing them as anything more than an attached detail. Perhaps the fine quality of her own, she reflected, was to do with her being an artist, a painter, albeit a strictly amateur one. She certainly preferred that to physical decline, to falling quietly ill. Consumptive, perhaps. On the threshold. She suddenly pressed her fist against her cheek, then heated it with her lips, as she had done with her two late and cherished twin nieces, who had turned into angels aged six, liberally scented with orange blossom powder.

William stopped and pointed up at the sky. He said he had spotted a species of broad-winged eagle. Louisa looked up, too, failing to find the bird. Within moments her knees were buckling. The rushing clouds had brought a giddiness that, completely to her surprise, seemed to be physically forcing her legs away from the vertical and towards some nebulous state that appeared attracted to the waves below.

But there was Dorothy's sudden, firm grip on her arm. The handrail was mostly air, its metal merely sketched on the empty vastness of creamy stuff beyond. Dorothy was the anchor, with her broad hands. Louisa was on her knees now, shaking. 'I am King Arthur's faithful steed,' she quipped, embarrassed, 'whose name I have forgotten.'

William rushed up but was similarly gripped by dizziness and had to sit down. She was relieved that someone else had been caught out by the place, its endless swaying and crashing. That it was solid rock made it worse. 'Dizziness is catching,' she said. But no one heard her, as the wind had started gushing through a rip in the rocks somewhat like a giant keyhole. The land had suddenly become little different from the sea. She felt ready to slide off into the plunging uncertainties all around them, despite the grip of her friend's hand.

Then suddenly there was Hugh.

'Shall we go back for tea?' he suggested, seemingly imbued with a new physical confidence. All that rugby, thought Louisa. The sweet, slow boy was a blessing, Louisa realised, if only for that single suggestion.

They began along the path towards warmth and refreshment and her companions seemed similarly relieved. She herself tried not to look anywhere but straight ahead, tasting the salt sprinkled on her cold lips from the endless churn below. Behind them the Cornishman trailed, clearly unable to comprehend them as they began again to natter and laugh like gulls over a putrid catch.

Not that the handsome *indigens* is the least bit interested in anything we say, Louisa reflected with a secretive smile that only Dorothy caught with a casual glance – and apparently failed to understand.

Myths, Legends and Folklore of English Heritage Sites

Charles Kightly

THE HISTORY OF ENGLAND includes that of its legends, myths and folklore, which tell us how people saw themselves and the world about them, of their fears, hopes and preoccupations. Below is a selection of these stories: those that relate directly to the legends and myths which inspired the authors in this collection, followed by others from across the country. English Heritage sites appear, at first mention in each section, in bold.

The Stories

'These Our Monsters'
NOT OF OUR WORLD

The tale of the Green Children of Woolpit – the Suffolk village whose name really does come from the 'wolf pits' once there – has two medieval sources. The longer and more detailed version was written in about 1198 by the Yorkshire chronicler William of Newburgh, who at first didn't believe it, until he was 'overwhelmed by the testimony of so many and such credible witnesses'. A slightly different variant was recorded during the 1220s by Ralph of Coggeshall, who was based nearer Woolpit at the Essex monastery of Coggeshall, and claimed to have known the family of Sir Richard de Calne, the knight in the tale.

One summer during the reign of King Stephen (1135–54),

villagers harvesting at Woolpit were amazed to discover two children, a boy and his sister, emerging from one of the pits they used for trapping wolves. Though otherwise resembling human children, they were dressed in clothes of a strange colour and unknown material, and their skin was completely green. They were clearly terrified when the Woolpit reapers seized them, but nobody could understand a word of their language. Many people came to see the amazing sight, and (says Ralph) they were taken as a curiosity to the manor house of Sir Richard de Calne, six miles away. At first starved (says William), they were offered bread and 'other victuals', but though 'tormented by hunger' they tearfully refused them. Then, happening to see some new-cut broad beans on their stalks, they eagerly grabbed them – but desperately sought for the beans within the stalks, not in the pods. When someone opened a pod for them, they gulped down the beans – and lived only on beans for months after.

Eventually they were baptised (presumably a precaution in case they were demons), and learnt both to speak English and to eat bread, gradually losing their green skin colour altogether. The boy soon died, but the girl, now 'differing not a bit from the women of our own country', lived for many years as a servant in Sir Richard's household, where (reported Ralph) 'she was rather loose and wanton in her conduct'. William was told that she married a man from King's Lynn, and was still alive a few years before he wrote, 'or at least, so they say'.

Often asked about her original homeland, she said that it was called 'Saint Martin's Land': it was a Christian country with churches, but wrapped in continual twilight, never getting lighter than just before dawn or just after sunset. Another, luminous, land could be seen from it, across a wide river. According to Ralph, not only the people but everything else in that land was green. When feeding their father's flocks there, the children heard chiming bells – like those of **Bury St Edmunds Abbey**, four miles from Woolpit. Then they were either suddenly carried in a trance to the Woolpit harvest field or led by the chimes into a cavern, from which they eventually emerged into the blinding light and warmer air of 12th-century Suffolk.

Among the most famous and intriguing of all English legends – if that is what it is – the story of the Green Children has given rise to endless speculation. The children have been 'identified' as (of course) lost extraterrestrials; leftover 'Ancient Britons'; refugees from one of medieval East Anglia's Flemish-speaking enclaves; sufferers from the deficiency disease chlorosis ('green sickness'); and a whole lot of other things. Some modern inhabitants of Woolpit (never actually named, naturally) are even said to be their direct descendants. As William of Newburgh tactfully ended his story: 'Let everyone say as he pleases, and reason on such matters according to his abilities.'

Stories about underground worlds not very unlike our own – the children's 'St Martin's Land' had churches, even if they were green – sometimes occur elsewhere in English as well as Scots and Welsh mythology. Another was told by William and Ralph's contemporary Gervase of Tilbury, in a book written to amuse his patron the German Emperor Otto IV, but scathingly dismissed by others as 'a bagful of old woman's tales'. It concerns dramatically sited **Peveril Castle** in the Peak District (one of whose 13th-century custodians, incidentally, is a possible candidate for Robin Hood's traditional enemy, the scheming Sheriff of Nottingham). Peveril is recorded in Domesday Book as the castle of 'Peak's Arse' after the vast cavern which lies almost beneath the spectacular castle crag. Also known as 'the Devil's Arse' (and now more politely as Peak Cavern), this sometimes emits mysterious winds and was long believed to be an entrance to Hell.

One bitter winter day, runs the tale, a swineherd working for the castle's lord lost a sow about to give birth to piglets, and guessed she'd taken refuge in the ominous cavern. Not daring to tell his master he'd lost such a valuable animal, he plucked up his courage and ventured in. After long wanderings through dark tunnels, he was amazed to find himself in a broad open country bathed in hot sunshine where reapers were busy harvesting. He soon found the sow and her new-born piglets and, meeting 'the lord of that land', was given permission to leave with them. Emerging on the castle crag, he found it still locked in midwinter.

Apart from the fact that the mysterious world beyond the Peak Cavern existed in the opposite climate – wishful thinking in midwinter Peveril, perhaps – there was nothing very alien about this underground world or its people. Back in medieval Suffolk, a much stranger quasi-human appears in another tale by Ralph of Coggeshall, this time set at newly completed **Orford Castle** during the reign of Henry II (1154–89). Fishermen working off the town caught in their nets 'a wild man', naked and rather bald but with a long beard and hairy chest. He couldn't or wouldn't speak, even when Bartholomew de Glanville, constable of the castle, strung him up by his feet and tortured him. He ate anything given him, squeezed the juice out of raw food. At first carefully guarded in the castle, he always slept from sunset to sunrise but, when taken into a church, showed no signs of religion or reverence. After a while they made him a place to swim in the sea, within a triple barrier of nets – he easily slipped under them, but came back of his own accord, staying in the castle for two months. Eventually his guards grew slack and he disappeared, never to be seen again. The chronicler didn't know what to make of him: was he really human, or a fish who'd taken on human shape, or an evil spirit hiding in the body of a drowned sailor? Despite some later depictions of him at Orford, he certainly wasn't a 'merman' with a fishlike tail: we're told he was strung by his feet.

The God-fearing villagers of Woolpit in 'These Our Monsters' would have been happier with the pious legends about 'our saint' – Saint Edmund of Bury St Edmunds Abbey. One of the very largest, wealthiest and most powerful monasteries in the country, it owed its name and prosperity to the burial there of the martyred Anglo-Saxon king Edmund of East Anglia. Edmund was the patron saint not only of the abbey, but also of medieval England, until displaced by the interloping St George. Defeated and captured in AD 869 by the invading Viking 'Great Army', Edmund refused to give up either his kingdom or his Christian faith. So the Viking leader Ivarr the Boneless had him tied to a tree and shot full of arrows. Ivarr then cut the 'blood eagle' in his back (bending the ribs away from the spine like an eagle's wings) and finally – while he still called on Christ – had his head hacked off. The severed head was then thrown into a dense thorn thicket, so that his followers couldn't find it. As they called out 'Where are you?', they heard a voice from the thicket replying 'Here, here, here'. They discovered the miraculously speaking head clasped between the paws of a great white wolf, which had piously guarded it against desecration. It followed them until Edmund's head and body were brought together, and then quietly vanished.

Though first recorded by Abbo of Fleury over a century after the event, the tale of St Edmund's miraculous head and the white wolf was based at two removes from an eyewitness account. Abbo heard it from St Dunstan, Archbishop of Canterbury (AD 909–988), who had himself heard it from a very old man, once Edmund's own young armour-bearer. He swore on oath that he'd been present on the fatal day and witnessed the wonder.

Medieval images of the wolf with Saint Edmund's crowned head survive in several East Anglian churches, including Bury St Edmund's Cathedral but not St Mary's at Woolpit – though there is a painting of the saint on the rood screen there. But it's the Green Children who have pride of place on the village sign. Today, Woolpit is rather proud of 'Our Monsters'.

'Great Pucklands'
PUCK AND THE FAIRIES

Great Pucklands meadow, where this story begins, really was surveyed for insects and flowers by Charles Darwin and his children in the 1850s. Though not then part of Darwin's gardens, it lies not far from the home of Charles Darwin, **Down House**, and was visible from his 'thinking path', the Sandwalk. Now in the care of English Heritage, Great Pucklands can be reached by a public footpath from Down House.

Like 20 or more other English places with similar names, Great Pucklands probably takes its title from 'Puck', the most famous of all English 'fairies'. Meaning 'devil' or 'evil spirit', versions of the name appear at a very early date not only in Anglo-Saxon but in Celtic and Scandinavian sources. He figures in Rudyard Kipling's well-loved children's novels, *Puck of Pook's Hill* (1906) and *Rewards and Fairies* (1910), and of course in Shakespeare's *Midsummer Night's Dream* (1595/6). Shakespeare's Puck, a rather sinister trickster, is nearer both in time and spirit to the Puck of folklore than Kipling's 3,000-year-old Sussex countryman. But neither has much connection with the Christmas-tree confections of Victorian and later fairy stories, which Kipling's Puck calls 'that painty-winged, wand-waving, sugar-and-shake-your-head set of impostors'. As Darwin says in the story: 'Fairies weren't always pretty mites. That was just tales people told for babies'.

The fairies of English folklore are much more unchancy and potentially dangerous beings, not to be trifled with. They could be child-sized, adult-sized or occasionally even bigger, and though they could fly if they liked, they never had wings. Visible or invisible at will, they usually lived underground, sometimes in large prehistoric burial mounds like Willy Howe in East Yorkshire, from which (the local 12th-century chronicler William of Newburgh records) a man stole a fairy cup. Unlike most illusory 'fairy gold', it didn't turn to leaves or ashes above ground, and still existed in William's time. And like those seen near **Housesteads Roman Fort**, fairies loved dancing; but any human drawn into their dance might be changed forever, or find 50 years had passed when they were released.

Though rarely really wicked, they delighted in playing tricks on humans. Puck's speciality was leading travellers round in circles until they were irreparably lost. At Aymestrey, near Leominster in Herefordshire, a man who'd been 'Puckled' in nearby Pokehouse ('Puck's House') Wood left a legacy to pay for the ringing of a church bell every evening, to guide fellow victims safely to the village. Much worse, fairies sometimes stole away human babies, substituting fairy changelings. And the mid-17th-century parish records of Lamplugh in Cumbria allegedly record three people 'frightened to death by fairies'.

But they could be kindly. When the Shropshire folk around **Mitchell's Fold Stone Circle** were suffering a famine, the fairies gave them a magic cow, whose milk sustained them until a wicked witch milked it dry. As a punishment she was turned into a stone, with a ring of standing stones set round her to keep her in. Fairies traditionally loathed witches, whom they regarded as trespassers on their magic territory.

They were indeed intensely touchy, especially about what people called them – like Kipling's Puck, they particularly disliked being called 'fairies'. Since they were often invisible eavesdroppers, it was always safest to call them, even behind closed doors, something like 'the good folk', 'the beautiful people' or 'the gentry'. As one fairy in a Scots poem warned a human:

If ye call me imp or elf
I warn you look well to yourself
If ye call me fairy
I'll work you much harm
If good neighbour you call me
Then good neighbour I will be

But if you call me 'seelie wight'
I'll be your friend both day and night.

'Seelie' means happy, blessed or lucky: but it comes originally from the Anglo-Saxon *saelig*, meaning 'holy'. 'Holy' in the usual sense fairies were not. Neither were they immortal, though much longer-lived than humans. Meeting 'fairy funerals' at night was a particular hazard in the English Midlands because those who saw them usually died soon afterwards. There was even believed to be a fairies' graveyard near **Brinkburn Priory** in Northumberland, some said housing fairies killed by hearing the priory bells ringing, to which they were notoriously allergic.

What then were they? Despite Annie's 'Equation' in the story ('Winged Insect – Winged Fairy – Hominin – Human'), they were not usually thought to be related to humans. The rare fairy–human marriages, like that of Anglo-Saxon 'Wild Edric' with a fairy maiden he met near **Clun Castle**, almost always ended tragically. Some medieval scholars guessed that they were really low-ranking rebel angels, cast out of Heaven together with Satan by Saint Michael. Not quite bad enough to descend with him to Hell, they'd got stuck halfway on 'Middle-Earth' (a term used many centuries before Tolkien made it famous). But what eventually happened to them? The 17th-century Anglican clergyman and wit Richard Corbet, who himself claimed to have once been 'Puck-led' on a journey, joked in his *Fairies' Farewell* that they were leftovers from the Roman Catholic 'Old Profession'. Tolerated in the easy-going pre-Reformation world, they'd then been banished by the stricter Christianity of the Puritans:

Witness those rings and roundelays
Of theirs, which yet remain
Were footed in Queen Mary's days
On many a grassy plain

But since of late, Elizabeth
And later, James came in
They never danced on any heath
As when the time hath been

By which we note the Fairies
Were of the old Profession.
Their songs were 'Ave Mary's'
Their dances were Procession
But now, alas, they all are dead;
Or gone beyond the seas;
Or farther for Religion fled;
Or else they take their ease.

The pioneering archaeologist John Aubrey, writing in about 1690, thought rather that the spread of literacy had 'put all the old fables out of doors, and the divine art of printing frightened away Robin Goodfellow (Puck) and the fairies'.

Darwin's own scientific theories, matured at Down House, must also have damaged belief in fairies. Yet tales about fairies (of the traditional, rather than the Victorian Christmas-tree variety) were still seriously credited well into the 20th century, especially in rural areas such as the Welsh Borders. And even now, and even in cities, one distant and degraded descendant of the alarming and powerful beings of folklore still maintains a precarious existence – the Tooth Fairy, first referred to in 1648.

'Goibert of the Moon'
HARE WITCHES AND THE HENGE

The teller of this story (and who'd dare to contradict him?) clearly knows a great deal about the international folklore surrounding the hare. He's aware that 'Hare-women are not always goddesses ... and they are not always benevolent ... many of the old suspicions that surrounded the hare in British folk culture seem to come from her association with the witch.'

Not all witch-hare stories date from the very distant past. One from near **Longtown Castle** in Herefordshire, recorded in 1909, relates that a witch in hare form was warned by her grandson: 'Run, grannie, run, the hounds be after thee.' Bitten by a hound as she disappeared through the keyhole of her cottage, she was of course found doctoring a wound in her leg. But not all witch-hares were caught, and some had fun with their pursuers. The most circumstantial account, 'affirmed a certain truth by many of the inhabitants ... upon their own knowledge', was told to the local MP Gervase Holles at **Bolingbroke Castle** in the 1630s. Before its demolition during the Civil War, local finance administrators held an annual meeting at the castle. But it was 'haunted by a certain spirit in the likeness of a hare, which at the meeting of the auditors doth usually run between their legs and sometimes overthrows [trips] them'.

Pursued into the castle courtyard, it disappeared into a cellar which had no means of escape ('not having the least chink or crevice'); yet though they 'most narrowly' examined every corner, the searchers could never find it. At other times they 'sent for hounds, and put them in after it, but after a while they have come crying out'. This Lincolnshire hare, tacitly assumed to be a witch who disliked tax collectors, was never tracked down – unlike the dancing hare in the story.

Though the storyteller instinctively feels that the dancing hare must somehow be connected with **Stonehenge**, recorded folklore makes no direct link between hares and the famous stone circle. Julius Caesar wrote in about 50 BC that Iron Age Britons regarded eating hares as taboo, but kept them as pets 'for amusement and pleasure'. Perhaps they were really more of a sacred or prophetic animal, since before her uprising in AD 60 Boudicca (Boadicea) released a hare from her robes, and rejoiced when it ran in a 'lucky' direction. But that was a very long time after Stonehenge had been abandoned, and many centuries before the first recorded stories about it began to appear.

Almost certainly the earliest account of Stonehenge was written by Henry of Huntingdon in about 1129, listing 'Stanenges' among the wonders of Britain, 'where stones of amazing bigness are raised in the manner of gateways, so that gateways seem to be set over gateways. Nor can anyone find out by what contrivance such massive stones were raised to so great a height, or for what reason they were erected there.' Less than a decade later, Geoffrey of Monmouth provided answers to both questions in his *History of the Kings of Britain*.

The British king Aurelius Ambrosius, Geoffrey tells us, wanted a new and distinctive building to stand forever as a memorial to Britons massacred by the Saxons. After a conference of masons and carpenters from across the land failed to produce any ideas, Aurelius was advised to consult Merlin, as renowned for his 'mechanical contrivances' as he was for true prophecies. If Aurelius wanted something really special, said Merlin, he should send for the Giants' Circle Dance (*Chorea Gigantum*) on 'Mount Killaurus' in Ireland (a circle of enormous stones which no man then living could erect) and set it up on Salisbury Plain.

How could such a massive structure, mocked Aurelius, be moved from a distant country? And weren't there enough stones in Britain big enough for the job? Annoyed, Merlin told him more about the Giants' Dance. Long ago, it had been brought by giants from the remotest corner of Africa, because it had mystic medicinal powers. Whenever the giants were ill, they poured water over its stones into baths, which would cure any disease: if mixed with certain herbs, such water would also heal all wounds.

Fired with enthusiasm, the Britons sent an army to Ireland to fetch the stones, and defeated an Irish force which tried to protect them. But when they got to Mount Killaurus, neither the strength nor the ingenuity of all the army's young men could shift the stones one inch. When he saw what a mess they were making of the task, Merlin laughingly set up his own gear (we're not told what this was) and dismantled the circle 'more rapidly than you would ever believe'. The stones were then carried on boats to Britain and set up on Salisbury Plain, arranged exactly as they'd been in Ireland. All this happened, Geoffrey estimated, in about AD 475 (actually Stonehenge was completed some 3,000 years earlier). Later, not only Aurelius but also his brother Uther Pendragon were buried within the circle.

Where did this extraordinary story come from? Mainly, no doubt, from Geoffrey's notoriously fertile imagination. Yet it does include some genuine history, and possibly a now-forgotten belief about the stones. Aurelius Ambrosius was probably a real person, though a Romano-British commander rather than a 'king', and some of Stonehenge's stones (the bluestones from the Preseli hills) were actually brought from far away, though from West Wales rather than Ireland. Astonishing engineering skills, equal to Merlin's, were indeed also needed to set up the original circle. It's also conceivable that water poured over the stones really was once believed to have healing powers.

Geoffrey's 'historical novel' – which also introduced the tale of Arthur's conception at Tintagel – was hugely popular and immensely influential. It remained the generally accepted account of Stonehenge's origins for over 500 years, with the variant that Merlin transported the stones from Ireland by magic (rather than, as Geoffrey says, using boats and his practical engineering skills).

Not until the early 17th century did alternative theories begin to appear. Scholars found it impossible to believe that the great monument could really have been built by 'Ancient Britons': Inigo Jones called them 'savage and barbarous people ... who squatted in caves, tents and hovels', and insisted instead that Stonehenge was Roman. Vikings, Phoenicians and (until it was proved that Stonehenge is older than Mycenae) Mycenaeans from Classical Greece were all in turn firmly identified as the real builders of the circle.

The 17th-century John Aubrey was much nearer the mark. He agreed that the ordinary Ancient Britons were only 'two or three degrees less savage than the Americans' – meaning what he would have called 'Red Indians' – but believed they also had a learned priesthood called the Druids. So for Aubrey, and in the 18th century for the influential researcher William Stukeley, Stonehenge became a Druid Temple. Though in reality the Druids flourished some 2,000 years after the circle was abandoned and had nothing to do with building it, they were at least British, and Aubrey's theory established the basis for research on Stonehenge that continues to this day. Any summary of it, to quote the title of Julian Richards's English Heritage publication, is only 'the story so far'.

In the face of these scholarly, though mistaken, theories, folklore took a back seat at Stonehenge. The exception was the legend that the stones couldn't be counted, which a series of celebrity stone-counters set out to disprove. On the run from Oliver Cromwell, the future Charles II found time to attempt the task in 1651; the diarist John Evelyn (having failed to break off a piece of monolith with a hammer) counted 95 stones in 1654; in the 1680s the matter-of-fact Puritan traveller Celia Fiennes, who had 'told [counted] them often', made their number 91. In the 18th century Daniel Defoe estimated 72 and William Stukeley 140 – both much farther off the now accepted total of 93 stones and fragments than their 17th-century predecessors.

Thus, Stukeley proclaimed, 'the magical spell is broke, which so long perplexed the vulgar'. Yet for many the spell of Stonehenge, and perhaps of its dancing hare, is not and never will be broken.

For more about the folklore of stone circles, see p.165.

'The Hand Under the Stone'
PETRIFIED SINNERS

Stone circles – like those which inspired this story – are the most perennially fascinating of prehistoric monuments. Though they exist in other parts of Europe and beyond, they're most numerous and most spectacular in the British Isles and Brittany. British circles date from between the middle Neolithic (New Stone Age) period, about 3300–2900 BC, and the early to middle Bronze Age, about 2200–1000 BC.

New discoveries about them are continually emerging, but it's now broadly believed that the fashion for stone circles began in the north and moved southwards. Thus, the circles on Orkney and the Hebrides are among the oldest in Britain, and the earliest in England are the circles of Cumbria, which Monny in the story knew best – including **Castlerigg**; remote but well-preserved Swinside; and Long Meg and Her Daughters. There's another grouping in the Derbyshire Peak District, including **Arbow Low** and the **Nine Ladies** (which Monny and her Aunty Ro visited). Midlands circles include **Mitchell's Fold** in Shropshire and Oxfordshire's **Rollright Stones**. And, more numerous than in any other English region, the circles of the South West include the vast and complex monuments at **Stanton Drew** in Somerset and, in Wiltshire, **Avebury** and, most famous of all, **Stonehenge**.

'In the region of Oxfordshire there are great stones arranged as if by the hand of man. But at what time, or by what people, or for what memorial or significance this was done is not known.' This anonymous 14th-century description of the Rollright Stones is quite exceptionally non-committal, resisting the compulsion to 'explain' such monuments which gripped most later observers. Often the interpretations mirror the preoccupations of the periods they belong to. Classically educated 17th- and 18th-century antiquarians such as John Aubrey and William Stukeley, having read Roman accounts of Druids, believed that stone circles were built as 'Druid Temples'. (This still-persisting notion is quite wrong, since the Druids flourished at least 1,000 years after the last circle was abandoned.) More recently, circles have been 'revealed' as the focus of mysterious 'ley lines' or landing places for aliens; as masterpieces of geometrical expertise, built using a measurement called the 'megalithic yard'; or (much more credibly, since some major circles are aligned to midsummer and midwinter sunrise) as sophisticated astronomical observatories. Today, again reflecting the preoccupations of the age, some suggest that stone circles were centres of prehistoric trading and commerce.

Folklore offered other explanations, among the most common being that the circles were people magically turned into stone, usually as a punishment for some sin. The most frequent offence was 'profaning the Sabbath' by dancing: the Nine Ladies, the **Nine Stones** (Dorset), the Merry Maidens (Cornwall), Long Meg and Her Daughters and many other circles were all women (it was generally women) petrified for offending in this way. At the complex monument of Stanton Drew, an entire wedding party was transformed. According to the most complete version of the story, a human fiddler refused to play beyond midnight on a Saturday, but the Devil himself took over, and the wedding party danced on into the Sabbath and its doom. Sometimes individual stones within or outside the circle have distinctive characters. At Stanton Drew they're the bride, groom, drunken parson and musicians, and at Long Meg and Her Daughters, where the outlier is much bigger than the rest of the stones and of a different material, it's Long Meg herself.

Other Sabbath-breaking crimes which merited petrification included the Cornish game of 'hurling', whose players became **The Hurlers**, and even the seemingly innocent children's game of fivestones, whose Sunday players (according to one version) became the Nine Stones, also endearingly known locally as 'Lady Williams and Her Little Dog Fido'.

Since most of these stories aren't recorded until Elizabethan times, some folklorists link them to a post-Reformation Protestant horror of Sabbath-breaking. But they could well be much older than that. Medieval clergy also strongly discouraged dancing on Sundays and holy days, and the earliest 'cursed dancers' legend originates from 11th-century Germany. Revellers who persisted (after due warning) in dancing in a churchyard beyond midnight on Christmas Eve were supernaturally compelled to dance there for a year without stopping. When most of them died of exhaustion, a ring of stones was set up to mark their graves.

Sabbath-breaking wasn't the only legendary reason for being turned to stone. It isn't now remembered what crime caused a band of 'carles' ('churls' or peasants) to be petrified into Castlerigg stone circle (alias 'the Carles'). But at Mitchell's Fold the transformed offender was a witch, who maliciously milked dry a fairy cow sent to succour people during a famine. The other stones in the circle were erected 'to keep her in'. At the Rollright Stones, a complex site whose three separate elements developed over the course of more than 2,000 years, it was a patriotic witch who did the transforming: meeting a king marching with his army to conquer England, she turned him into the King Stone; his army became the King's Men stone circle; and his conspiring courtiers the Whispering Knights chambered tomb. And Celia Fiennes, who visited Long Meg and Her Daughters in 1698, gave another reason than the usual dancing for their punishment: the Daughters (or Sisters), she says darkly, were rumoured to have been transformed for 'soliciting Great Mag to an unlawfull love'.

A no-nonsense Puritan, Celia had scant regard for legends. She didn't think much of the stone circle, which she thought had really been erected simply to warn travellers that the surrounding area was marshy. As for the tale that the stones couldn't be counted, that was pure nonsense: there were obviously not more than 30. In fact there are 69. Others took the widespread taboo against trying to count the stones in a circle more seriously. At Castlerigg and Swinside, the Hurlers and Stanton Drew, it was believed to be impossible to count the stones so as to get the same result twice, and at Stanton Drew an 18th-century investigator was warned that he might be 'struck dead on the spot' if he tried to sketch them. Stonehenge, the Hurlers, the Rollright Stones and the 'Countless Stones' of **Little Kit's Coty House** (the fragments of a chambered tomb rather than a stone circle) all share the tale of a baker who tried to count the stones by putting a penny loaf on each, and then calculating how many of a numbered batch he had left. But either the Devil gobbled up the loaves as they were placed, or the baker fell dead before he could announce the result. At Long Meg and her Daughters, as so often with this site, one legend's different: if you can count the stones correctly twice over, and then put your ear to Long Meg, you'll hear her whisper secrets. As Monny in the story did.

If counting the stones was hazardous, trying to move or destroy them could be fatal. One labourer who did so at **Mayburgh Henge** in Cumbria went mad, and another hanged himself. When one of the Rollright Stones was used to bridge a stream, it took 24 horses to shift it and a man was killed in the process. Every night it flipped itself back onto the stream bank, crops failed and when eventually the unlucky stone was replaced, just one horse was sufficient to haul it. At Avebury (an immensely impressive site but oddly lacking in folklore) deliberate burial or breaking up of the great stones was done at intervals from the 14th century into at least the 18th, without recorded mishap. But in 1938 the body of a 14th-century barber-surgeon (identified and dated by coins and instruments in his purse) was discovered under a fallen stone. It was understandably concluded that he'd been crushed when undermining the stone. Recent re-examination of the body suggests that he was already dead when he was buried there. But who or what killed him?

Few now (it's to be hoped) would think of moving or damaging such stones. Conversely, leaving offerings to them at the solstices and other significant times (as Aunty Ro and the 'hippies' in the story did) is increasingly common at many sites, including the Nine Stones. Yet there (again echoing Monny's story) rival groups of neo-pagans have protested strongly against this 'desecration'. With stone circles, you can't be too careful.

For more about the folklore of Stonehenge, see p.160.

'The Dark Thread'
VAMPIRES AND THE UNDEAD

The major inspiration for the popular modern vampire craze is the novel *Dracula*, written in 1897 by the Irish author and theatre manager Bram (Abraham) Stoker (1847–1912). As in 'The Dark Thread', it takes the form of a series of letters, diary extracts and newspaper articles. In the story Count Dracula travels in an earth-filled coffin from his castle in Transylvania (in modern Romania) to Whitby. He is a vampire who, being dead, needs the blood (the life force) of the living to survive. So he drains to death all the crew of his ship and, after landing at Whitby, makes a victim of Lucy Westenra, luring her to a graveyard by night and biting her neck. Thus transformed into a vampire herself, Lucy begins to prey on children, until her former friends behead her, stake her through the heart and fill her mouth with garlic. Dracula himself is pursued to Transylvania and finally defeated by having his throat cut and a knife driven through his heart.

Dracula is a completely fictional character, whose links with **Whitby Abbey** are entirely imaginary. This needs to be emphasised, because the world's most famous vampire has made Whitby the Goth capital of England, and some visitors to the dramatic abbey ruins still have to be convinced that he didn't really operate there. Bram Stoker was certainly inspired by holiday visits to Whitby, as well as (so he later claimed) by a nightmare he had after eating too much Whitby crab meat. But Dracula himself springs mainly from the eastern European vampire legends Stoker studied, and possibly from tales of the bloodsucking Irish *dearg due* heard in his youth. The Transylvanian vampire has little to do with English folklore.

Little, but not nothing. Serious English folklorists are scornful about vampires and it's certainly true that the word 'vampire' (or 'vampyre') doesn't appear in the English language until the 1730s. Like many of the trappings of the classic vampire – stakes through the heart, garlic, contagious vampirism – the word comes from eastern Europe. Yet tales of 'revenants' or 'the Undead' (the original title of *Dracula*) do exist in English folklore. In these, exceptionally wicked men are given power by the Devil to rise from their graves after death – not as shadowy spectres, but walking corpses – to trouble and even kill the living. Probably the earliest such story in England, datable from internal evidence to the mid 12th century, was recorded by the courtier Walter Map (*c*.1135–1210) and takes place in Herefordshire. A Welsh sorcerer died unrepentant, but his undead corpse rose from the grave every night, individually summoning his fellow villagers by name, whereafter they invariably died within three days. So many perished that the village became almost depopulated and the desperate local squire, a knight called Sir William Laudun, appealed to Bishop Foliot of Hereford for help. Dig up the corpse, ordered the bishop, cut off its head with a spade, then soak it in holy water and rebury it. This didn't work, and the revenant summoned Sir William himself: but the valiant knight chased it back to its grave with drawn sword and as it was descending into the ground he sliced its head in half. After that, there was no more trouble.

Other medieval tales about the undead originate from much nearer Whitby. Some are told by William of Newburgh, who came from Bridlington and spent his life at Newburgh Priory near Coxwold, both about 40 miles away from Whitby.

Writing in about 1198, he complained that 'walking corpses' were a fairly common 'nuisance' in his time; he had space only for four of the many stories about them. The most horrifying – allegedly related to William by an eyewitness – involved a runaway Yorkshire miscreant who fled to (probably) Alnwick in Northumberland. There he died unconfessed after falling from the roof-beam over his wife's bed, where he'd been spying on her frolics with a lover. Despite Christian burial, his corpse rose from the grave and roamed the town nightly, followed by a pack of dogs. It beat anyone it met 'black and blue' and, worse still, its 'pestiferous breath' infected the whole town with deadly plague, so that the surviving inhabitants fled. Eventually two sons of a plague victim went to dig up the corpse, which they found just below the surface, 'swollen to an enormous corpulence, with its face suffused with blood'. Struck by a spade, it spewed out such a flow of gore that it seemed like a monstrously engorged leech. They dragged it to a fire and, after tearing out its heart, burnt the 'baneful pest' to ashes – whereupon the plague immediately ceased.

Two centuries later, in about 1400, another revenant was reported from **Byland Abbey**, a few miles from William's home and, again, not very far from Whitby. It's among an extraordinary series of 12 very matter-of-fact ghost tales recorded by an anonymous Byland monk, who even provides the undead's name in his account: the body of James Tankerlay, rector of 'Kereby' (probably Cold Kirby), was honourably buried in the abbey's chapter house. But it took to wandering back to Kereby by night and eventually 'blew out' the eyes of Tankerlay's former mistress. Instead of chopping up, decapitating or burning the corpse in the usual way, the Byland authorities had it dragged, coffin and all, to nearby Lake Gormire and thrown in, though the oxen pulling it nearly died of fright.

The most striking evidence for medieval Yorkshire belief in the undead, however, emerged only in 2017, when archaeologists investigated pits at **Wharram Percy Medieval Village**.

These pits were separate from the churchyard where villagers were normally buried, yet they held the jumbled remains of about ten people, including a teenager, two women, and two infants aged between two and four, deposited at various times between the 11th and 13th centuries. Surprisingly, many displayed clear signs of having been deliberately beheaded, chopped up or partly burnt *after* death. The most likely explanation for this treatment, the archaeologists concluded, was that these were people who the villagers suspected of 'walking' after death. If this interpretation is true (and there are other possibilities), then Wharram was plagued not only by female and teenage vampires as well as the usual adult male revenants, but even by undead toddlers.

Though there's no evidence in history or folklore for the undead in Whitby itself, the town and abbey have legends of their own. The local tales of Abbess Hild of the (still-performed) Penny Hedge ceremony and of alum entrepreneur Thomas Chaloner mentioned in 'The Dark Thread' are all genuine, though only the fevered imagination (or a surfeit of Whitby crab sandwiches) of the character of Stoker in the story can produce a dark thread of vampirism in them. There's also a myth about the abbey bells, allegedly carried off by ship when Henry VIII dissolved the abbey in 1539. At the earnest prayer of the outraged townspeople, the ship inexplicably sank in a flat calm off Black Nab, where on calm nights the submerged bells can still be heard ringing.

The most famous Whitby legend concerns the historical Abbess Hild, the seventh-century Anglo-Saxon princess-turned-abbess who rid the headland monastery of an infestation of poisonous snakes. Wielding a 'holy or magical wand', she drove them over the cliff, and in the fall they smashed their heads; her prayers then miraculously turned them to stone. This accounts for the fossilised ammonites – resembling coiled snakes to the eye of faith – still sometimes found on Whitby's beaches, and which still figure in the town's heraldic arms. A formidable woman, honoured, respected and feared by kings, churchmen and commoners alike, Hild would surely have been more than a match for Dracula, if he had ever existed.

'Breakynecky'
REDCAPS AND HOBGOBLINS

The background to this story is the partial demolition of the ruins of medieval **Berwick Castle** in 1847–50 to make room for the new railway station. Its platforms now stand on the site of the castle's great hall. Stone from the castle was also used for the station and the majestic Royal Border Bridge over the Tweed, still used today by London–Edinburgh trains. About a third of the 'navvies' who did the work were Irish, many of them (like Séan in the story) refugees from the Great Hunger, the potato-blight famine which killed about a million Irish people between 1845 and 1849. Among the few remains of the castle they left is the steep and dangerous medieval stairway, which once linked the castle to its riverside jetty, called the Breakneck Steps – 'Breakynecky'. The redcap in the stories told by the modern teenagers was a goblin who killed people by dropping stones on them; Séan died when a stone from Berwick Castle fell on his head.

Redcaps are probably the most vicious and dangerous creatures in Anglo-Scottish folklore. Haunting ruined Border castles, they look like short, thickset old men with long protruding teeth, skinny fingers with nails like eagle's talons, fiery red eyes and straggly grey hair. Shod in iron boots, they carry a staff with an iron spike and wear a distinctive red cap. If travellers are unwary enough to shelter in their lair, they kill them with stones, and then refresh the dye in their red cap by soaking it in their blood. Too powerful to be vanquished by human strength alone, a redcap can be driven off (by Protestants) by reciting verses from the Bible or (by Catholics) by brandishing a crucifix. He will then utter a disappointed howl and vanish in flames, leaving a large tooth behind him. Rather like a tooth-fairy in reverse.

A redcap called 'Fatlips' was believed to haunt the ruins of Dryburgh Abbey, but the most notorious of the breed was Robin Redcap or Redcap Sly, who lived in a triple-locked chest at the sinister castle of Hermitage in Liddesdale. As much a witch's familiar spirit as a goblin, he protected the wicked black magician Lord William de Soulis against his enemies, until Soulis broke the taboo against looking at him, whereupon he vanished. Soulis's vengeful neighbours were then able to capture him, wrap him in a sheet of lead and boil him to death in a cauldron at Ninestane Rig stone circle. Lord William was a real person, who actually died while in prison for conspiring against King Robert the Bruce. But the boiling makes a better story.

These redcaps are from the Scottish side of the Border, and tales of English redcaps are harder to find. But since they were traditionally attracted to fortresses where blood had been shed and injustices done, there's no lack of English candidates, Berwick Castle being the clear front runner. Originally a prosperous Scottish Border town, Berwick changed hands no less than 13 times during the long Anglo-Scottish wars, often after bloody sieges. On Good Friday 1296 Edward I of England took the town and proceeded to massacre its inhabitants, even though they'd submitted to him. According to the 15th-century Scots chronicler Walter Bower, he 'spared no one, whatever their age or sex. For two days streams of blood flowed from the bodies of the slain, for in his tyrannous rage he ordered 7,500 souls to be massacred ... So that the town's watermills could be turned by their blood.'

Edward I was also largely responsible for building Berwick Castle, which became the key to the eastern end of the Border. Superseded in the 16th century by the up-to-date bastioned ramparts which make Berwick one of the most impressive fortified towns in Europe – they're worth going a long way to see – the old castle had fallen into ruin long before Séan and his comrades cannibalised it for the railway station.

Away from the Border and its redcaps, northern England was infested by the much less dangerous beings called hobs, hobgoblins or hobthrushes. Some lived wild in natural caves or, like the alleged inhabitant of **Hob Hurst's House** ('Hobthrush house') in the Derbyshire Peak District, in ancient prehistoric burial mounds. But more attached themselves to houses and families, invisibly doing farm or domestic work by night and achieving more than any ten people could do, in return for the occasional bowl of cream. Like their relations the 'boggarts' and 'brownies', however, they were very easily offended, and then everything around the house was sure to go wrong.

Probably the most famous hob was 'the Cauld Lad' of **Hylton Castle** in Tyne and Wear, where English Heritage care for a splendid, heraldry-bedecked, late medieval gatehouse which is all that remains of a once much larger mansion. Bound to the place by a spell, the Cauld Lad could often be heard lamenting:

Wae's me. Wae's me
The acorn's not yet fallen from the tree
That's to grow the wood, that's to make the cradle
That's to rock the bairn, that's to grow to a man
That's to lay me

Though he tidied up overnight anything left untidy, he also perversely messed up any room already left in order, throwing plates about and breaking pots. Eventually the exasperated servants decided to get rid of him. Following the traditional procedure for 'laying' hobs, they set out a suit of green clothes for him; if he accepted them, he'd have to go. Joyfully crying out:

Here's a cloak and here's a hood

The cauld lad o'Hylton will do no more good
the hob vanished forever.

Other versions of the story, however, insist that the Cauld – or 'cold' – Lad was not a hob at all, but the unquiet ghost of a servant boy. He'd either died of cold when locked in a cupboard or been murdered by a lord of Hylton and dumped in a pond, where it was said a boy's skeleton had been found. In 1609, Robert Hylton of Hylton Castle was indeed pardoned for killing one Roger Skelton with the point of a scythe at harvest time – allegedly by accident. According to this version, moreover, the Cauld Lad wasn't banished, but in early Victorian times could still be heard wailing in a room in the castle. Even a wailing ghost, however, was surely preferable to a murderous redcap.

'The Loathly Lady'
THE ARTHURIAN LEGENDS

The story of the Loathly Lady and her marriage to King Arthur's handsome knight Sir Gawain was a great medieval favourite. This retelling is based on a poem called 'The Wedding of Sir Gawain and Dame Ragnell', written in the mid 15th century. It's just possibly by Sir Thomas Malory, more famous as the author of the great Arthurian story-cycle *Le Morte Darthur* (*The Death of Arthur*), originally called *The Whole Book of King Arthur and His Noble Knights of the Round Table*. It's only one of many versions, and the tale and the character were already so well known by the 13th century that (according to a slightly dubious chronicler) a squire dressed up as the Loathly Lady was a star turn at the entertainments celebrating Edward I's second marriage in 1299. Which is rather ironic, since the battle-scarred king was over 60 at the time, while his bride, renowned for her beauty, was just 20.

At the end of the 14th century John Gower retold the story in his *Confessio Amantis* (*The Lover's Confession*), and his much more famous contemporary Chaucer used it in his *Canter-*

bury Tales as 'The Wife of Bath's Tale'. In Chaucer's version, however, the man who seeks the answer to the story's central question, 'what do women want?', is a knight condemned to death for rape, who is eventually reprieved by Guinevere and ladies of Arthur's court when he provides the 'right' answer. But what was the 'right' answer? All the medieval versions agree that what women wanted was 'sovereignty' or 'mastery' – which is to say domination:

> *We desire of men above all manner of things*
> *To have the sovereignty of all both high and low*

says the Dame Ragnell version, while the Chaucer story says:

> *Women desire to have sovereignty*
> *As well over her husband as her love*
> *And for to be in mastery him above*

That's the *public* medieval answer, which saves Arthur (and Chaucer's knight) from death. But in private, in all the medieval variants, it's Gawain's offer of 'choice' which breaks the spell on the Loathly Lady, making her beautiful both day and night. The subtle, or not so subtle, difference in Fiona Mozley's modern retelling is that both the public and the private answers are the same. What women most want is not domination, but choice.

The story is set around Carlisle in Cumbria, a region which Sir Gawain knew well, having already completed an arduous quest there. The retelling's 'Gawain has experience of bargains struck, of twelve-month promises, and the honest proffering of a neck for a woodsman's axe' is a sly reference to another great medieval poem, 'Sir Gawain and the Green Knight'. Contemporary with Chaucer's work, it's nothing like as well known, because it's written in a north-western dialect, much further removed from modern English than Chaucer's

'London' speech. In it Gawain journeys alone through the 'wilderness of the Wirral', assailed by dragons, giants, wild woodwoses and terrible winter weather:

Ner slayn wyth the slete he sleped in his yrnes
Mo nyghtes then innoghe in naked rokkes
[*Nearly killed by the sleet, he slept in his armour*
More nights than enough in the bare rocks]

He's seeking to meet the Green Knight and fulfil a promise to take a return blow from him, in recompense for a stroke dealt by Gawain a year earlier at Arthur's court.

There's no room to tell the rest of that tale here – it's well worth seeking out and reading for yourself. But it's a reminder that north-west England, and Cumbria in particular, has a strong claim to be Arthur's homeland – though Cornwall, Wales, Somerset, lowland Scotland and several other parts of Britain would violently dispute that. As its name shows, Cumbria was not originally English territory: it's related to *Cymru* and *Cymry*, the Welsh-language titles for Wales and the Welsh. All three names come from the Romano-British word '*combrogi*' meaning 'fellow countrymen' or 'fellow (Roman) citizens' – fellow Britons who, like Arthur, held out against the Anglo-Saxon invaders. The fact that the forest where the tale of the Loathly Lady begins is called Inglewood – 'the wood of the English' – is further evidence that the English were the exception thereabouts. You wouldn't need to single out a wood in, say, Anglo-Saxon Wiltshire as belonging to the English, because all woods there did.

Certainly Cumbria preserves many Arthur legends. **Carlisle Castle** (not actually begun until the 11th century, but on the site of a Roman fort later taken over by Romano-British Cumbrians) is identified by several medieval Arthurian tales as Arthur's 'Camelot'. (Though that's a claim hotly contested by Colchester – once Camulodunum; Cadbury Castle in

Somerset; and Caerleon in south Wales.) At least two Cumbrian sites were known as the Round Table of the legendary king. One, now lost, was a Roman amphitheatre near Carlisle. The other, **King Arthur's Round Table**, is in Eamont Bridge near Penrith. Henry VIII's travelling historian, John Leland, who visited it in the early 1540s, says it was 'by some called the Round Table, and by some Arthur's Castle'. In fact it's a circular prehistoric earthwork 'henge' monument, perhaps much later used as a medieval jousting arena: when you're visiting it, don't miss the still more spectacular Neolithic **Mayburgh Henge**, a short walk away.

Ravenglass Roman Bath House, which in reality served the adjacent Roman harbour-fort of Glannoventa, has more ambitious Arthurian claims. Still probably the tallest surviving Roman building in northern England, it was known in Elizabethan times as Walls Castle, and thought to be a medieval fortress, the palace of King Everlake the Unknown, legendary King of Avalon. Here, according to some stories, the body of the mortally wounded Arthur was brought, and from there carried across the (Irish?) sea by seven queens, to be healed and to await his moment to return.

But that's another point at issue. Other legends insist that Arthur and his knights lie sleeping underground somewhere in Britain, awaiting their recall at the time of the nation's greatest need: one suggests in a cave beneath **Richmond Castle** in Yorkshire and another near **Sewingshields** crag on **Hadrian's Wall**. Wherever they lie, Sir Gawain seemingly isn't with them. According to Malory, he was badly wounded in the head in single combat with Sir Lancelot and then unluckily struck again on the old wound in a battle against the forces of the wicked Mordred at Dover. He died in **Dover Castle**, and was buried in the castle chapel. As triumphant proof of this story, says Malory, 'there all men may still see the skull of him, and the same wound is seen that Sir Lancelot gave him in battle.'

What was firmly believed to be Gawain's skull was indeed displayed at Dover Castle for well over a century. The Spanish tourist Ramon de Perellos viewed it there in 1397 and in 1485 William Caxton (who not only wrote a preface to Malory's tales of Arthur, but also, crucially, printed them for the first time) cited it among other surviving Arthur relics as proof that the legendary king had once really existed. Leland reported that the skull was still on show in the 1540s. But after that little more is heard of it. Does a relic of Dame Ragnell's wisely choosing and (eventually) delighted husband still survive in a forgotten corner somewhere?

'Capture'
TRISTAN AND ISEULT

The inspiration for this story, the legend of Tristan and Iseult (or Isolde or Yseult), is not quite as Louisa retells it. Shorn of many additions over the centuries, the core legend tells that Tristan is the nephew of King Mark of Cornwall, who lived at Tintagel. A slayer of dragons and monsters, Tristan is also an accomplished falconer and musician. He's sent to Ireland to bring home his uncle's chosen bride: Iseult, daughter of King Anguish. Supremely beautiful, she's also renowned as a healer. But on the way back Tristan and Iseult both drink (either deliberately or by mistake) a magic love potion which has been prepared for Iseult and Mark's wedding night. So Tristan and Iseult fall hopelessly in love. Iseult marries Mark all the same, but continues to love Tristan in secret. Eventually Mark finds out, and Tristan reluctantly gives up Iseult and goes into exile in Brittany. There he marries (confusingly) another Iseult, called 'of the White Hands', but is wounded by a poisoned arrow. Only the original Iseult can save him with her healing skills, so he sends to Cornwall for her. Her ship is to fly white sails if she is aboard, black if she's not. Iseult comes, but Tristan's jealous new wife tells him the ship has black sails and he dies of despair. Iseult then dies of a broken heart. Mark allows the doomed lovers to be buried side by side at Tintagel, where a vine and a rose tree intertwine over their graves.

Tintagel Castle has been inspiring legends for many centuries. Their foundation is the fact that 'Din Tagell' – meaning 'the fortress with the narrow entrance', describing the headland-and-island site perfectly – really was an important power centre of Cornish rulers between about AD 450 and AD 650. During this post-Roman, Early Middle Ages (sometimes called 'the Dark Ages'), pagan Anglo-Saxons progressively conquered much of what is now England. But in the South West the old Romano-British kingdom of Dumnonia – Cornwall, Devon and part of Somerset – long held out, maintaining the Christian faith and (as a recent discovery at Tintagel proves) the ability to speak and write Latin and Greek.

Other archaeological finds from Tintagel prove that its princely inhabitants enjoyed both direct seaborne links with Europe and a high standard of living. These include the biggest assemblage of imported Mediterranean pottery tableware found in western Britain; wine and olive-oil jars from as far away as Greece, Turkey and North Africa; and luxury glassware from France and Spain. Naturally almost impregnable, the island fortress also had a plentiful source of fresh drinking water, allowing it to be defended against enemies who may have included Irish colonists as well as raiding Saxons.

For reasons now unknown, Tintagel had largely been abandoned by about AD 700. But memories of its past glories long survived in legend, probably reinforced by the physical remains of its early medieval buildings. Still visible today, these must have been much more apparent in the 1100s, when the Tintagel legend industry began moving into higher gear. So much so that during the 1230s Richard, Earl of Cornwall, brother of Henry III and one of the richest men in Europe, built a strategically useless but highly symbolic castle here, staking his claim to a place in the Tintagel story.

The legend that Earl Richard bought into, and today is

much the best known of the Tintagel myths, was first written down in about 1138 by the wildly successful 'historical novelist' Geoffrey of Monmouth. His *History of the Kings of Britain* tells how Uther Pendragon, King of Britain, fell in love with the beautiful Ygraine, wife of Duke Gorlois of Cornwall. To protect her from Uther's lust, Gorlois locked her up in the strong fortress of Tintagel, which half a dozen men could defend against an army. But the enchanter Merlin magically transformed Uther into the exact likeness of Gorlois: in this disguise he passed unhindered into the fortress and slept with Ygraine, who thus conceived the future King Arthur. Where the famous hero was actually born we aren't told, but for many Tintagel is (albeit without even legendary evidence) hailed as Arthur's birthplace.

Though the Arthur legend has now swept the board at Tintagel, it is the story of Tristan and Iseult that has the longest association with, and the best historical claim on, the site. The oldest surviving versions of the story were written down in France (by one 'Thomas of Britain') and Germany in the mid 12th century. But these were all but certainly based on earlier legends from Cornwall, Brittany, Wales and Ireland, 'Celtic' lands bound together by the sea routes between them. Breton stories at least as old as the ninth century record a King Mark, also called Cunomorus (meaning 'hound of the sea'), who ruled not only in Cornwall but also in Brittany. He allegedly died in battle there, near the significantly named Ile Tristan, in about AD 560. Iseult's Irish father, 'King Anguish', was also probably a historical figure, the famous King Aengus of Munster.

More concrete (or in this case granite) evidence that Mark/Cunomorus and Tristan were real Cornish rulers survives about 28 miles south of Tintagel, near Fowey and nearer the hillfort of Castle Dore, once thought to be the site of King Mark's court. Here a sixth-century standing stone is inscribed in Latin: 'Here lies Drustanus, son of Cunomorus'. Some believe that 'Drustan' is 'Tristan', in which case he was the son, not the nephew, of King Mark. So their shared relationship with Iseult, if it happened, becomes even more transgressive and poignant.

And there's more. According to the admittedly unreliable testimony of Henry VIII's historian John Leland, who saw the Drustan Stone in about 1536, the epitaph on it then ended 'with Lady Ousilla' – a Latinisation of the Cornish name 'Eselt', not so far from 'Iseult'. So does Iseult also lie here with her lover (and stepson?) rather than at Tintagel as in the legend? There are a lot of 'ifs' here. But it's certain that, just as the Arthur legend took over Tintagel from the older myth of Tristan and Iseult, the once separate and independent tale of the doomed lovers also got sucked into the all-conquering Arthur story-cycle. As early as the 13th century, Tristan had been demoted from a Cornish–Breton prince to a mere Knight of the Round Table.

Other Sites and Other Stories

The Jewel Tower
LONDON

Sole survivor of the royal apartments within the great medieval palace of Westminster, the Jewel Tower was built in about 1365 to safeguard Edward III's personal treasures. But it was raised on confiscated monastic land (belonging to Westminster Abbey), something which folklore insisted was almost guaranteed to bring bad luck. Worse still, its foundations disturbed the grave of a holy hermit. A monk of injured Westminster Abbey later gleefully recorded the terrible punishment inflicted on the chief instigator – William Usshborne, Keeper of the King's Privy Palace. First, Usshborne plotted with a local leadworker to dig up the hermit, throw his bones into a pit and steal the lead from his coffin: but when the leadworker got the coffin to his workshop, 'all strength departed from his body', and he soon afterwards died.

Usshborne didn't take this heavy hint. Instead he created a fishpond in the Jewel Tower moat, and invited his neighbours to dine on a pike taken from it. 'But as soon as he had swallowed two or three mouthfuls of the fish ... he began shouting "it is trying to choke me!" ... and suddenly he fell to the ground and died a wretched death without the last rites' (thus, according to medieval belief, almost certainly bound for Hell). 'It was said', the monk smugly went on, 'that this happened because he had confiscated the meadow and garden of the infirmary and the prior of Westminster's garden for the use of King Edward III. For this, there was absolutely no compensation to the church of Westminster.'

Dover Castle
KENT

Another story of supernatural retribution was reported from Dover Castle in the 1950s. It's a tale about a solitary roadside sycamore tree just visible from the castle battlements, possibly told originally by garrison soldiers. The tree marked the spot where, at some unknown date, a Dover soldier beat a comrade to death with a sycamore-wood club. He then stuck the club in the ground, boasting cynically to himself that his crime wouldn't be discovered until the dry stick took root. The murderer was posted abroad, and many years passed before he returned to the scene of the crime. To his horror, he found that the murder weapon had indeed miraculously taken root, and grown into a flourishing sycamore tree. Struck with remorse by this sign of divine judgement, he confessed to the murder, and was hanged. Sycamore trees do grow quickly – a sapling can reach ten feet high in its first year. But nobody now seems to know where the ominous tree stood, or whether it's still there.

Kit's Coty House
KENT

More clearly visible, Kit's Coty House near Aylesford in Kent was among the very first English monuments to be officially protected (in 1883) by the state. It's actually a prehistoric chambered tomb with three huge sarsen stones (sandstones from the chalk downs of southern England) topped by a massive capstone; raised about 4000 BC, it was originally covered by a 'long barrow' earth mound. Learned Elizabethan scholars such as William Camden, however, got its date wrong by 3,000 years. They maintained that 'Kit's Coty' was 'Categirn's Coty' – the tomb of the British prince Categirn, son of Vortigern, killed by the Saxons in about AD 450 – and that the nearby **Little Kit's Coty House** was the grave of his Saxon rival Horsa, brother of Hengist, also slain at the nearby and genuinely historical Battle of Aylesford.

Folklore told a different story – that Kit's Coty was built by three local witches, who had to call in a fourth to summon up enough magic power to lift its huge capstone. Others, more prosaically, held that Kit's Coty just meant 'Kit's cottage', where Kit the shepherd boy sheltered with his sheep. But it's apparently still believed that if you place anything on Kit's Coty at full moon (difficult, since the monument is protected by railings) and then walk round it three times, the object will disappear.

Minster Lovell Hall
OXFORDSHIRE

A better-authenticated tale about a disappearance relates to Minster Lovell Hall in Oxfordshire. This was once the home of Francis, Lord Lovell, notorious (or renowned, according to your point of view) along with Ratcliffe and Catesby as a leading henchman of Richard III – the White Boar (in reference to his heraldic device) or, more insultingly, 'the Hog':

The Rat, the Cat, and Lovell our Dog
Rule all England under the Hog

Escaping Richard's defeat at Bosworth, Lovell fought on against Henry VII, landing at **Piel Castle** in 1487 with the Yorkist pretender Lambert Simnel. When Simnel was in turn defeated at Stoke Field, Lovell again escaped – some believed he was drowned during his flight, but another story, recorded in 1622, held that 'he lived long after in a cave or vault'. So it was perhaps no surprise when, in 1708, workmen breaking through a wall at Minster Lovell discovered a secret room. It contained the body of a dead man – Lord Lovell surely – sitting at a table with a dead dog at his feet. But as soon as fresh air rushed in, bodies and table instantly crumbled to dust.

Though it was reported on very good authority, there are all sorts of problems with this story – one of several in folklore where walled-up bodies suddenly turn to dust on discovery, which bodies don't really do. Not least is the question of whether anyone hiding in a secret chamber would take a potentially barking dog with him. Lovell certainly did survive the Battle of Stoke, being recorded living in Scotland in June 1488. But what happened to him in the end isn't known. Perhaps 'Lovell our Dog' – and his own dog – really did finish up at home in Minster Lovell Hall.

Silbury Hill
WILTSHIRE

The biggest artificial prehistoric mound in Europe, awe-inspiring Silbury Hill was raised in about 2400 BC, and clearly played a crucial, though now unknown part in the **avebury** 'sacred landscape'. Its purpose is unknown, but it certainly isn't a burial mound. Though it's been tunnelled into both vertically and from side to side, and thoroughly investigated by English Heritage in 2007–8, no burial has ever been found there. Folklore knows better. 'Zel-bury Hill' (the old local pronunciation) is the burial place of King Zel, who was interred there on horseback, and the mound was magically raised over him in the time it took to boil a pan of milk. So John Aubrey heard in 1670, and it was later told that Zel was buried in a golden coffin, and could sometimes be seen riding round the hill in golden armour; or that the 'body' buried was actually a life-sized solid gold statue of a horse and rider. Zel is fictitious, and a more plausible theory was offered for the mound by the 18th-century pioneer antiquarian William Stukeley, who suggested that Silbury might be a memorial to the anonymous builder of **Avebury Stone Circle**. Another, quite different story linked the great mound to the 'Druids' or 'priests' of Avebury. When the Devil planned to bury the town of Marlborough (or in some versions **Stonehenge**, or Avebury itself) under a massive sackful of earth, the priests stopped him in his tracks by their magic. He dropped his sack and its contents became Silbury Hill.

Old Sarum
WILTSHIRE

The spectacular Iron Age ramparts of Old Sarum enclose the remains of a Norman castle and a great cathedral, all that's left of the city where William the Conqueror once gathered all the nobles of England. But the hilltop site was an uncomfortable place to live. The water supply was poor, high winds sweeping round the cathedral drowned the priests' services, and the clergy quarrelled bitterly with the soldiers in the neighbouring castle. So, in about 1220, Bishop Richard Poore decided to build a new cathedral in a more hospitable setting.

In fact the site of the present 'New Salisbury' cathedral was chosen for purely practical reasons, but folklore tells another story. The bishop, it relates, ordered an archer to shoot an arrow from Old Sarum's ramparts, or some say he shot the arrow himself. Where it fell, he built Salisbury Cathedral.

But there's a problem with this tradition. Salisbury Cathedral is only just under two miles (3,200m, or 3,520 yards) from Old Sarum. But the greatest distance a highly trained professional medieval archer (let alone a middle-aged bishop) could shoot the lightest 'flight arrow' was only 370m (or 400 yards) – about an eighth of the actual distance from the ramparts of Old Sarum to the cathedral site. Medieval people, much more familiar with archery than we are, must have been aware of this discrepancy, which suggests the story is a late one. Persistent folklorists get round the difficulty. The arrow, they explain, actually hit and wounded a passing deer, which ran on until it finally dropped dead where the cathedral now stands, still stuck with the arrow.

Hailes Abbey
GLOUCESTERSHIRE

Renowned for 'the Holy Blood', allegedly a portion of Christ's blood shed at the Crucifixion, Hailes Abbey in Gloucestershire was among the most famous pilgrimage destinations in medieval England. It was founded in 1246 by the immensely wealthy Richard, Earl of Cornwall, brother of Henry III and nominal 'King of the Romans', in thanksgiving for deliverance from a shipwreck. Richard, an Arthurian-myth enthusiast who also built **Tintagel Castle**, was buried at Hailes in 1272, two years after his son Edmund gave the abbey the sensational relic from which its fame and prosperity sprang. Edmund bought this phial of the Holy Blood (perhaps part of the regalia of the ninth-century Emperor Charlemagne) while travelling in Germany. He gave a third of it to Hailes, the other two-thirds going to the monastery of Ashridge in Hertfordshire; but it was at Hailes that the relic, and the stories and pious legends surrounding it, chiefly burgeoned.

In the 14th-century *Canterbury Tales* Chaucer's rascally con man the Pardoner swore 'by the blood of Christ that's now at Hailes'. But most of its votaries were more pious, touching their rosaries against the rock-crystal globe that enshrined it and being relieved if they could see it clearly – which only those whose sins had been forgiven could do. Other (probably abbey-promoted) tales about the relic discouraged doubters: one priest who dissuaded his parishioners from visiting it saw the communion wine in his chalice boiling, another found his service-book bleeding.

Rich gifts to Hailes and its famous relic continued right up until Henry VIII's break with Rome in 1534, whereafter the doubters came into their own. Inclined to Protestant reform, Anne Boleyn enquired into the 'abominable abuse' of pilgrimages to Hailes, and in 1538 the relic was publicly denounced as nothing more than 'the blood of a duck or drake, regularly renewed'.

Others declared it was actually clarified honey coloured with saffron. It was taken to London and destroyed; magnificent Hailes Abbey was closed down, and soon afterwards enthusiastically pillaged, mainly by the local people whose pride it had been a few short years earlier.

Okehampton Castle
DEVON

The largest castle in Devon, Okehampton is allegedly the scene of a nightly supernatural penance. The ghost of Lady Mary Howard, allegedly murderous wife of the equally dubious Sir Richard Grenville, sets out from Fitzford Manor in a coach made of human bones, driven by a headless coachman. It's accompanied by a great black dog, either headless or with a single glowing eye – some say the hound itself is Lady Howard. It drives 16 miles across the moor to Okehampton Castle mound, where the dog plucks just one blade of grass. Then it returns to Fitzford, where the grass is placed on a stone, and the spectral procession vanishes – until the next night. The penance won't be completed until the castle mound is bare of grass; and that will never happen, because the grass grows more quickly than the hound can pluck it.

This popular story is still told, and perhaps believed, in Okehampton. In some versions Lady Mary is condemned to her torment for murdering the first three of her four husbands, in others for disinheriting her children. But it's also been suggested that the legend is a case of mistaken ghostly identity. Its 'Lady Howard' is not the locally infamous Lady *Mary* Howard, but the even more nationally notorious Lady *Frances* Howard. This scandalous Jacobean courtier was alleged to have bewitched her first husband into impotence, and was certainly instrumental in poisoning Sir Thomas Overbury, who opposed her second marriage, with arsenic-tainted tarts and a mercury chloride enema. But who, unfortunately, had nothing to do with Okehampton.

Leiston Abbey
SUFFOLK

Terrifying phantom hounds, generally black and sometimes headless, but usually with big, glowing saucer-eyes, appear in folklore from all over England. The most renowned in literature is Conan Doyle's *Hound of the Baskervilles*. Set on Dart-moor, his story was probably inspired by a local legend of the squire who sold his soul to the Devil, and after death continued to hunt with a pack of black hounds.

But the demon dog's favourite haunts seem to be in East Anglia, where he's known as Old Shuck, from the Anglo-Saxon *scucca*, meaning devil, and often has a '*shucky*' (shaggy) coat. He's recorded there as early as 1127, when 'jet black dogs with eyes like saucers were seen by all the country' among a spectral Wild Hunt which appeared for over forty successive days between Peterborough and Stamford.

His most spectacular East Anglian manifestation, recorded in a popular pamphlet called 'A Straunge and terrible Wunder', was at Bungay in Suffolk on Sunday, 4 August 1577. He burst into the crowded parish church of St Mary during a violent storm, breaking the necks of two parishioners 'in one instant' and shrivelling up another 'like a piece of leather scorched in a hot fire'. On the same stormy day he also appeared in Holy Trinity Church, Blythburgh, killing another three people and leaving scorch marks on a door, still shown to visitors.

Stories about Old Shuck remain widespread in East Anglia. He can be kindly, guarding women on lonely roads, guiding lost travellers, or (according to a Norfolk report in 1988) even saving them from rogue car drivers. But more often 'the Hateful Thing' is an omen of death and disaster. So there was great excitement in May 2014, when archaeologists working near the impressive monastic ruins of Leiston Abbey in Suffolk discovered the wellpreserved skeleton of a huge male hound. It would have weighed about 90kg, and stood an alarming 2m high on its hind legs. It had been buried long after the suppression of the abbey, but radiocarbon dating of the bones wasn't precise about exactly when: it may have been in 1650–90, 1730–1810 or even after 1920. The local press, of course, speculated that this was Old Shuck. But it couldn't have been. As a demon dog, Shuck doesn't die, and besides (if recent stories are true) he's still appearing in East Anglia.

Binham Priory
NORFOLK

Almost every ancient building worth its salt is rumoured to conceal secret passages. Several stories (for instance from **Richmond Castle** and **Netley Abbey**) recount the sad fate of adventurers who've tried to penetrate them. At Binham Priory in Norfolk (notable for its splendid nave, still in full use as the parish church) the passage supposedly led to nearby Walsingham Priory, or alternatively to **Blakeney Guildhall.** Its course was patrolled above ground by a ghostly black monk, who seemed to be searching for something. Perhaps he was one of several mad or wicked characters from Binham's unusually troubled history: one prior squandered the priory's treasures to pay for alchemical experiments, another died raving and was buried in chains.

The story goes that a local fiddler, Jimmy Griggs, with his dog Trap, rashly volunteered to explore the passage, fiddling all the way so that his friends on the surface could trace his progress. But when they reached Fiddler's Hill the music suddenly stopped and Trap came dashing out yelping. Jimmy Griggs was never seen again, and some said the phantom monk had collared him.

Fiddler's Hill is actually a prehistoric burial mound at a crossroads. When roadworks cut into it in 1933, two human skeletons – thought to be Bronze Age or Anglo-Saxon – were found, along with the skull of an animal. These were immediately hailed locally as the remains of the fiddler, the monk and Trap, 'proving' the legend's truth. In fact one of the skeletons was that of a girl, and the animal skull may have been a goat's – and anyway Trap supposedly escaped. But facts should never spoil a good story.

Waltham Abbey
ESSEX

The burial place of the last Anglo-Saxon king, Harold God-winson, has never been firmly established. Rival stories began to emerge soon after his death at the Battle of Hastings in 1066. One was that William the Conqueror refused to hand the body over to Harold's mother, despite her offer of its weight in gold; instead, he had it buried by the Sussex seashore, with an epitaph mocking Harold's failure to guard the coast against the Normans. But the priests of Waltham Abbey in Essex insisted that the king's naked and mutilated corpse was identified on the battlefield by his mistress Edith Swan-Neck, by 'certain secret marks' only she knew. It was then taken for burial at Waltham, where a gravestone in the abbey grounds marks its resting place.

Harold had certainly rebuilt the abbey of Waltham Holy Cross in 1060, allegedly in thanks for being miraculously cured of paralysis by its famous relic. This 'holy cross', a black marble crucifix, was discovered in Somerset in about 1016 by a blacksmith led to it by a dream. When 24 oxen were harnessed to the cart carrying it they refused to move until the name 'Waltham' was spoken, after which they drew it of their own volition the 150 or so miles to the Essex church. 'Holy Cross' was the English battle-cry at Hastings, where Harold died.

Or did he? Within a century of 1066, tales that he'd survived spread, growing ever more elaborate. Badly wounded, he'd been taken to Winchester and secretly nursed back to health by a 'Saracen woman'. Then he'd wandered around English shrines for many decades as a nameless pilgrim, until divinely directed to St John's Church in Chester. There (aged over 100) he'd confessed his identity to Henry I in 1121, died and been buried. It was even claimed that his body was rediscovered there in 1332, still showing no signs of corruption – one of the indications of sanctity.

Stokesay Castle
SHROPSHIRE

Shropshire's Stokesay Castle is the finest surviving fortified medieval manor house in England. It's encircled by hills, the most prominent being View Edge to the west and Norton Camp to the east. On these two hilltops, according to a legend recorded in the 19th century, lived two giants, probably brothers, who kept their shared money in a locked chest in the castle vaults. They also shared a key to the chest. If one wanted it and the other had it, he shouted to his brother on the opposite hilltop to throw it across. But one day a throw fell short, and the key dropped into the (then water-filled) castle moat. Both giants searched for it, but never found it, and nobody has found it since. So the giant's locked treasure chest still stands somewhere under the castle. Even if anyone finds it, they can't break in, because it's guarded by the 'great big raven' sitting on it and the key remains lost. And, ends the story, 'many say it never *will* be found, let folks try as much as they please.'

Leigh Court Barn
WORCESTERSHIRE

Though comparatively little-visited, Leigh Court Barn in Worcestershire is an amazing triumph of medieval carpentry. Over 42m long, 11m wide and 9m high, it's the biggest timber cruck-framed structure anywhere in Britain. Built for the monks of Pershore Abbey, medieval owners of the manor of Leigh, it's now believed to have been raised in about 1345.

According to legend, a phantom coach drawn by four fire-breathing horses used to be seen flying up and over the barn, before disappearing into the nearby river Teme. It was driven by the spirit of 'Old Colles', condemned to do so for a highway robbery. Desperate for money, he had ambushed by night a friend carrying bags of gold, seizing the horse's bridle to stop him. But the friend drew his sword and cut off the grabbing hand. It remained attached to the bridle, and was immediately recognised as Colles's hand by a distinctive signet ring. Though his friend forgave him, Colles soon died of the wound. But his ghost drove the coach until 12 parsons were gathered to exorcise it with bell, book and candle. The spirit couldn't rise again until the last inch of candle burnt out. So the parsons threw the stub into a pond, where it could never be relit, and to make doubly sure filled in the pond. And, said local people: 'peaceful ever after slept Old Colles's shade.'

Old Colles was very much a real person – Edmund Colles, whose family had long administered Leigh manor for the Pershore monks, and acquired it for themselves after the Dissolution of the Monasteries. His grandfather had been 'a grave, wise and learned' judge, but young Edmund, 'being loaded with debts which like a snowball from Malvern Hill gathered increase', was forced to sell the family manor to a wealthy outsider from Suffolk, Sir Walter Devereux. Perhaps his breaking the ancestral ties of ownership (as with the phantom coach-driver at **Okehampton Castle**) was the real reason for his punishment, rather than highway robbery. Unusually, you can still see effigies of the characters in this story – the judge, Sir Walter and Old Colles himself, the eldest kneeling son on his father William's monument – in nearby Leigh church.

Lincoln Medieval Bishop's Palace
LINCOLNSHIRE

Tucked away in the shadow of Lincoln Cathedral, Lincoln Medieval Bishop's Palace was once the focus of the largest diocese in England, stretching from the rivers Humber to the Thames. The oldest part of the palace, the east hall, was built by the most famous and universally beloved of all Lincoln's medieval bishops – Saint Hugh.

Hugh of Avalon (not the mythical Arthurian island of Avalon, but his birthplace in Burgundy) became bishop in 1186. 'Fearless as a lion in any danger', he stood up to violent anti-Jewish mobs of stay-at-home crusaders in Lincoln and Northampton and defied Plantagenet kings, treating Richard the Lionheart 'like a naughty child' and always fiercely defending the rights of ordinary people. He could also defy convention, once biting off two fingers from the supposed hand of St Mary Magdalen he was shown in Normandy and bringing them to Lincoln as a relic. If he could chew the body of Christ Himself at holy communion, he reasoned, why not the bones of a saint?

Hugh's funeral at Lincoln in 1200 attracted one of the biggest crowds ever seen, with King John helping to bear his coffin. Twenty years later he was canonised, and pilgrims flocked to his two shrines in the cathedral, one housing his body and the other his head. When thieves stole the jewelled head reliquary, but then took fright and dumped the skull in a field, a black crow stood guard over it until it was found. Many other stories emphasise Hugh's power over wild creatures. He kept squirrels as pets, and befriended a shy wild whooper swan which appeared at his palace at Stow near Lincoln; it would eat from his hand, and guarded him when he slept, attacking anyone who came near him. It was clearly seen to mourn his death, and remains St Hugh's emblem today.

Thornton Abbey and Gatehouse
LINCOLNSHIRE

Comparatively remote but once very wealthy, Thornton Abbey in north Lincolnshire has an utterly astonishing 14th-century gatehouse, bedecked with turrets, sculpture and carved figures. As the local antiquarian Abraham de la Pryme put it in 1697, it's 'of a vast and incredible bigness and of the greatest art, ingenuity, and workmanship that I ever saw in my life'.

Abraham also tells us why so little remains of the other abbey buildings. They were deliberately pulled down in about 1607 by the newly rich Sir Vincent Skinner to furnish material for his 'most stately hall' on the site; 'which hall, when it was finished, fell quite down to the bare ground without any visible cause, and broke in pieces all the rich furniture that was therein'. Cannibalising monastic buildings was notoriously unlucky, but Thornton's buildings were unluckier than most. Even when its stones were taken away for buildings elsewhere – a sluice on the Humber and a mansion in Thornton Curtis – these too fell down 'by the just judgement of God'.

The antiquary likewise heard that, about a century before his visit, workmen had found a room containing a monk sitting at a table with pen, book and paper, 'all which fell to ashes when touched'. William Stukeley, who visited in 1722, was told a similar story. Tales of walled-up monks, like unlucky ruins, are almost standard elements of monastic folklore, but this one has a twist: later writers believed that the walled-up monk was Abbot Thomas Gresham, who really did build Thornton's magnificent gatehouse in the 1380s. Though revered immediately after his death as a miracle-worker, Gresham seems subsequently to have developed a reputation as a black magician, for which he was allegedly punished by walling-up.

Sadly, we may never know more. For the portion of the manuscript Thornton chronicle recording his life was deliberately torn out by some anonymous busybody in the 17th century; 'to prevent, as he sayd, the scandal of the church. The truth is the account given on him was that he was a wicked man, a Sodomite and wot not.'

Burton Agnes Manor House
EAST RIDING OF YORKSHIRE

Standing beside magnificent Jacobean Burton Agnes Hall in East Yorkshire – a privately owned mansion, but open to the public – is what looks like a sash-windowed early Georgian brick building. But this facade hides the core of the medieval Burton Agnes Manor House, with its lovely 12th-century vaulted undercroft and a 15th-century upper floor.

Here, while the new Hall was being built in 1598–1610, lived the three daughters of Sir Henry Griffith. All were agog to see the new mansion completed, but none more than the youngest, Anne. Before that happened, sadly, Anne was attacked and mortally wounded by robbers. As she lay dying, she made her sisters promise to cut off her head after her death and keep it in the new Hall 'as long as it shall last'. Instead, they buried her complete body in the churchyard.

When the family moved into the Hall, however, mysterious groans and strange noises made the place uninhabitable. No servant would stay. So after two years of this torment they dug up and decapitated Anne, setting her skull on a table in the house. All was then well, unless any attempt was made to oust the skull: when an unbelieving maid threw it onto a passing waggon, the horses went wild and the whole house shook. Eventually the Boynton family (who succeeded the Griffiths and whose descendants still live in the Hall) had it bricked up somewhere in the house walls, so that it could never be moved again. If the present owners know exactly where it is, they don't tell. But some say that 'Owd Nance', as she was known in the village in the 19th century, still (rather perversely) haunts a bedchamber in the Hall.

Wheeldale Roman Road
NORTH YORKSHIRE

Visible amid high moorland near Goathland, this enigmatic milelong stretch of stone trackway is part of 'Wade's Causeway', a much longer but now hard-to-trace route extending both northwards and southwards. Usually identified as a Roman road, it may rather be prehistoric, medieval or not a road at all but a Neolithic boundary marker.

Folklore has the answer. The Wheeldale Roman Road was of course built by the giant Wade and his giant wife, Bell, either to link their respective homes at Mulgrave Castle and **Pickering Castle**, or to help Bell reach and milk her (giant) cow as it grazed the moorlands. Bell brought the stones and Wade hammered them in. Many other prehistoric or natural features hereabouts are also attributed to Wade and Bell.

Stone cairns mark where Bell tripped and spilt aprons-full of road stones, and stone monoliths are boulders hurled about in tantrums by Wade as a giant baby.

Here reduced to rural domesticity, the giant warrior Wade once figured in more heroic legends from all over northern Europe, and may have originated as a Baltic sea-god. Giants like him were also thought responsible for other inexplicable ancient structures in the English landscape: describing the ruins of a Roman town, an eighth-century Anglo-Saxon poet called them '*enta geweorc*' – the work of giants.

Beeston Castle
CHESHIRE

Visible for many miles around, Beeston Castle crowns a high sandstone crag towering over the Cheshire Plain. On the very summit is the inner bailey, enclosing the famous castle well, which, at over 100m (328ft) deep, is among the deepest in any English castle. From at least the 18th century this well has been believed to conceal a great treasure. Some say it was hidden there by Royalists during the epic Civil War siege of 1644–5. But most maintain that it was concealed by Richard II in 1399, shortly before he was captured in north Wales and eventually murdered by Henry Bolingbroke, afterwards Henry IV. It's valued suspiciously exactly at 100,000 marks (£66,000) in gold coins and the same amount in precious objects (including jewelled badges of Richard's white hart emblem).

Richard may indeed have hidden valuables at Beeston during an unrecorded (but possible) visit in 1399, as he more certainly did in 'water cisterns' in other places around this time. But the same contemporary sources which record this also note that Bolingbroke's agents soon recovered the hidden treasures.

Neither this fact, nor the belief that anyone who searches for it will be struck dumb or driven mad by its guardian demons, has deterred many determined efforts to find the treasure. The well was investigated in 1794, again in 1842, in 1935–6, in 1976 and more recently in 2009 using cameras. There are at least three openings off the well shaft, one a nine-metre-long tunnel apparently leading nowhere. But no treasure has yet been found, and no-one has yet been struck dumb or gone mad. That we know of.

Lindisfarne Priory
NORTHUMBERLAND

Lindisfarne Priory is among the most atmospheric of English Heritage sites, all the more so because the 'holy island' on which it stands can be reached only at low tide. It's redolent of the memory of St Cuthbert, greatest of the saints of northern England. Here he reluctantly served as prior of the Anglo-Saxon monastery, before retiring to live as a hermit on still more inaccessible Inner Farne Island. There his turf-built oratory was sunk and walled so that vistas of sea or land could not disturb his contemplation of God. Buried in the priory in ad 687, his body was transferred to a new shrine 11 years later, and found to be untouched by corruption, a sure sign of sanctity. Later driven from the island by Viking raids, the monks carried the relics through many wanderings, eventually enshrining them in what became Durham Cathedral.

St Cuthbert's life (and afterlife) inspired numerous legends, many about his relationship with animals. When he was hungry, on one occasion an eagle dropped a fish into his boat; on another his horse (which he called his comrade) miraculously found a meal for him concealed in the thatch of a cottage. (It would be impious to suggest that this was somebody's workaday lunch.) On both occasions, he shared the meal with the provider. After he'd been praying naked in the sea – something the resolutely ascetic saints of the 'Celtic' tradition were much given to – two otters were seen to dry his feet with their breath and to warm him with their fur. To medieval hearers, such legends didn't so much show that the saint was kind to animals: rather that, like St Godric of **Finchale Priory** and St Hugh of Lincoln, Cuthbert's holiness was so great that all God's creation instinctively served him.

The saint's well-attested protection of eider ducks nevertheless chimes with modern (though totally un-medieval) principles of conservation. Still relatively common on the Northumbrian coast, and still known in local dialect as 'Cuddy's (Cuthbert's) Ducks', these striking birds shared the saint's Farne Island retreat, even tamely nesting beside his oratory's altar. Cuthbert decreed that they should never be killed, eaten or disturbed, posthumously backing up his prohibition by fatally striking down monks who disregarded it. They were, however, permitted to harvest the highly valued 'eider down' from nests after the ducks had used and abandoned them. Cushions of 'Cuthbert down' were among the most prized possessions of the saint's Durham Cathedral shrine.

Sewingshields Wall
NORTHUMBERLAND

Sewingshields crag on the Whin Sill ridge, just over a mile from **Housesteads Roman Fort**, is one of the best places to view **Hadrian's Wall**. A cavern under the nearby (but now vanished) border fortress of Sewingshields Castle was one of several places in northern England where King Arthur and his knights were believed to lie sleeping. The Sewingshields version of the legend has a nice local touch. A shepherd was sitting on the castle ruins knitting – hand-knitted long stockings were produced by Border and Yorkshire Dales shepherds until well into the 20th century – when his ball of wool disappeared into an underground passage. Pursuing it, he found a vaulted chamber lit by magic fire, where the king and his retinue lay in enchanted slumber, accompanied by a pack of hounds. A sword, a garter and a horn lay on a table in their midst. Being well-versed in legend, the shepherd knew enough to use the sword to cut the garter. But when the sleepers began to rouse he took fright, sheathed the sword and failed to blow the horn. Before sinking back into unconsciousness, Arthur just had time to declaim:

O woe betide that evil day
On which this witless wight was born
Who drew the sword, the garter cut
But never blew the bugle-horn.

And, of course, the terrified shepherd either couldn't remember or wouldn't tell where the entrance to the passage was.

A very similar story was told about a vault under **Richmond Castle** in Yorkshire (where dithering 'Potter Thompson' failed even fully to draw the sword). There's also a highly coloured variant version from **Dunstanburgh Castle**, complete with flaming-haired enchanter, two giant skeletons and a living maiden trapped in a crystal tomb. Drawn mainly from the lurid imagination of the best-selling Gothic novel writer 'Monk' Lewis, this doesn't specifically identify the sleeping warriors as King Arthur's knights. And the penalty for choosing the offered horn rather than the sword was that 'Sir Guy the Seeker' lost the maiden forever.

Most stories about the sleeping king and his knights agree that they are awaiting summons at the hour of England's greatest need. So, if they really had been awakened at Sewingshields (or Richmond) by a chance-come horn blower, wouldn't that have been somewhat premature? But this is to apply logic to folklore, something we should never do. And perhaps, after all, that is why the king and his knights have yet successfully to be woken.

Biographical Notes

Edward Carey

Edward Carey is a writer and illustrator whose books include *The Iremonger Trilogy: Heap House*, *Foulsham*, and *Lungdon*; *Observatory Mansions*; and *Alva & Irva: The Twins Who Saved a City*. His artwork has been exhibited in Florence, Collodi and Milan in Italy; in Kilkenny, the Republic of Ireland; in London, UK; and Austin, USA; his essays and reviews have been published in *The New York Times*, the *Guardian*, the *Observer*, *Corriere della Sera*, *la Repubblica*, and other places. His most recent novel, *Little*, about the early life of Madame Tussaud, has been sold in 16 countries. A new novel, *Fish House*, about the two years that Geppetto, Pinocchio's father, spent inside the whale, will be published in 2020. He is currently working on his eighth book, probably about a hospital filled with monsters.

Alison MacLeod

Alison MacLeod's most recent book, the short story collection *All the Beloved Ghosts*, was shortlisted for the Edge Hill Short Story Prize 2018 for best single-author short story collection in the UK and Ireland. It was also a finalist for Canada's 2017 Governor General's Literary Award for Fiction and named one of the *Guardian* 'Best Books of 2017'. In 2016, MacLeod was joint winner of the Eccles British Library Writer's Award. Her most recent novel, *Unexploded*, was longlisted for the 2013 Man Booker Prize and serialised for BBC Radio 4. It is currently optioned for film, while her short stories are often heard on BBC radio. MacLeod is a citizen of both Canada and the UK, and is currently at work on her next novel in Brighton, her adopted city.

Paul Kingsnorth

Paul Kingsnorth is the author of two novels, two collections of poetry and three works of non-fiction. His debut novel, *The Wake* (2014), was longlisted for the Man Booker Prize and won the Gordon Burn Prize. It is set during the almost-forgotten, decade-long war of underground resistance which spread across England after the Norman Conquest of 1066 and is written entirely in Kingsnorth's interpretation of Old English, recreated for modern eyes and ears. He is co-founder of the Dark Mountain Project, a global network of writers and artists producing work for the age of ecocide. He is also founder of the Wyrd School, a peripatetic wild writing academy in the west of Ireland, where he lives.

Sarah Hall

Sarah Hall is the author of five novels and three short story collections. Her work has been translated into more than a dozen languages. *Haweswater* (2003) was winner of the Commonwealth Writers Prize for Best First Novel, *The Electric Michelangelo* (2004) was shortlisted for the Man Booker Prize, *The Carhullan Army* (2007) was winner of the John Llewellyn Rhys Prize, *How To Paint A Dead Man* (2009) was longlisted for the Man Booker Prize and winner of the Portico Prize for Fiction and *The Wolf Border* (2015) was shortlisted for The Southbank Sky Arts Awards and the James Tate Memorial Black Prize, and winner of the Cumbria Life Culture Awards Writer of the Year prize. Her first collection of short stories, *The Beautiful Indifference* (2011), won the Portico Prize for Fiction and the Edge Hill Short Story Prize and the lead story, 'Mrs Fox', of her second collection, *Madame Zero* (2017), won the BBC National Short Story Award in 2013.

She is an honorary fellow of Aberystwyth University and the University of Cumbria, a fellow of the Civitella Ranieri Foundation and a Fellow of the Royal Society of Literature. She has judged a number of prestigious literary awards and is a recipient of the American Academy of Arts and Letters EM Forster Award. She was born and raised in Cumbria and currently lives in Norwich.

Graeme Macrae Burnet

Graeme Macrae Burnet was born and brought up in the industrial town of Kilmarnock in Ayrshire and now lives in Glasgow. In 2013 he won a Scottish Book Trust New Writers Award and in 2017 was named Author of the Year in the Herald Scottish Culture Awards.

He is the author of three novels: *The Disappearance of Adèle Bedeau* (2014), *His Bloody Project* (2015) and *The Accident on the A35* (2017). *His Bloody Project* was shortlisted for the 2016 Man Booker Prize and the LA Times Mystery Book of the Year and won the Saltire Prize for Fiction and the Vrij Netherlands Thriller of the Year Award. It has been published in 22 languages and variously described as 'astonishing', 'fiendishly readable' and 'spellbinding'. He is currently working on his fourth novel.

He is fond of black pudding, donkeys, train stations, trashy Euro-pop, mongrels and autumn.

Sarah Moss

Sarah Moss is a Fellow of the Royal Society of Literature and the author of six novels and a memoir of a year in Iceland: *Names for the Sea*, which was shortlisted for the RSL Ondaatje Prize 2013. Of her novels *Night Waking* (2011) was one of the eight winners of the Fiction Uncovered Prize, *Bodies of Light* (2014), *Signs for Lost Children* (2015) and *The Tidal Zone* (2016) were all shortlisted for the Wellcome Book Prize, and her latest, *Ghost Wall* (2018), was longlisted for the Women's Prize for Fiction and the Gordon Burn Prize and shortlisted for the RSL Ondaatje Prize and the Polari Prize. Her work is translated into 15 languages. She was born in Glasgow, grew up in Manchester and after moving between Oxford, Canterbury,

Reykjavik and Cornwall now lives in Coventry, where she is Professor of Creative Writing at the University of Warwick.

Fiona Mozley

Fiona Mozley's first novel, *Elmet*, was published in 2017 by John Murray Originals. It was shortlisted for the Man Booker Prize, the Ondaatje Prize and the Sunday Times Young Writer of the Year Award, and was longlisted for the Women's Prize for Fiction and the Dylan Thomas Prize. It won a Somerset Maugham Award and the Polari Prize. Mozley has written for the *Times Literary Supplement*, the *New Statesman*, the *Guardian*, the *Financial Times* and British *Vogue*. She was born in East London, raised in York, and has lived in Cambridge and Buenos Aires. She now lives in Edinburgh and is completing a PhD in Medieval Studies at the University of York. Her second novel will be published by John Murray in 2020.

Adam Thorpe

Adam Thorpe was born in Paris in 1956 and began his career as a mime. He is the author of 7 books of poetry, 11 novels, 2 collections of stories, 2 works of non-fiction, a stage play, many radio plays and broadcasts, and numerous reviews. His work has been translated into many languages and his translations of Flaubert's *Madame Bovary* (2011) and Zola's *Thérèse Raquin* (2014) were published by Vintage Classics. In 2007 he was shortlisted for the Forward Poetry Prize, the BBC National Short Story Award and the South Bank Show Award for the year's best novel (*Between Each Breath*). *Hodd* (2009), a dark version of the Robin Hood legend, was shortlisted for the Sir Walter Scott Prize for Historical Fiction in 2010.

Thorpe's first novel, *Ulverton* (1992), received the Winifred Holtby Memorial Prize and was dramatised for BBC Radio 4. It was described by Karl Ove Knausgård, author of *My Struggle*, as his 'favourite English novel' and 'a brilliant, very, very good and very unBritish novel … It's magic, a magic book.' Thorpe's non-fiction, *On Silbury Hill* (2014), was chosen as Radio 4's Book of the Week. Hilary Mantel has recently written: 'There is no contemporary I admire more than Adam Thorpe.'

ILLUSTRATIONS, INTRODUCTION AND AFTERWORD
Clive Hicks-Jenkins

Clive Hicks-Jenkins is an artist renowned for his explorations of folklore and mythology. Fresh from illustrating the 2018 Faber & Faber edition of Simon Armitage's *Sir Gawain and the Green Knight*, he was commissioned by English Heritage to create the visual styling of their interactive 'Map of Myth, Legend & Folklore', launched online in the spring of 2019. Working in collaboration with the Bristol-based digital agency Gravitywell, the artist produced all the artwork and animations for the map, and afterwards continued with the theme by making illustrations for a range of publications commissioned by English Heritage. The year 2019 marked the publication of three books illustrated by the artist: *These Our Monsters* for English Heritage, Simon Armitage's *Hansel & Gretel: a Nightmare in Eight Scenes*, published by Design for Today, and *The Book of the Red King* by the American poet Marly Youmans, published by Phoenicia.

James Kidd

James Kidd is a freelance writer based in Oxford. His writing has appeared in *The Independent*, the *Literary Review*, the *Observer*, *Esquire*, the *Daily Telegraph*, the *South China Morning Post*, *The National* and *Time Out*, among others. He hosts *This Writing Life* podcast (thiswritinglife.co.uk), featuring interviews with writers such as Hanya Yanagihara, David Mitchell, Michel Faber and Karen Joy Fowler, and co-hosts *Lit Bits* (litbits.co.uk), named by the *Observer* as one of its top three literary podcasts. He also works for the Keats-Shelley Memorial Association, which looks after the Keats-Shelley House in Rome.

Charles Kightly

Charles Kightly lives in the East Riding of Yorkshire and in Radnorshire in the Welsh Marches. A professional historian, he has particular interests in the late medieval period (the period of his PhD) and the 17th century. He is currently historical editor of the English Heritage Members' Handbook and has also written two English Heritage Red Guides. His numerous publications include *Folk Heroes of Britain* (1982); *Country Voices: An Oral History of Rural England and Wales* (1984); *Customs and Ceremonies of Britain* (1986) and *The Perpetual Almanack of Folklore* (1989). He has overseen the recreation of historical interiors in many buildings in Wales, England, Belgium and Scotland. A trustee of several charities, he has been an Anglican churchwarden for 30 years.